Sarpanch Sahib

Changing the Face of India

Edited by
Manjima Bhattacharjya

HarperCollins *Publishers* India
a joint venture with

New Delhi

First published in India in 2009 by
HarperCollins *Publishers* India
a joint venture with
The India Today Group

The Hunger Project is a global strategic organization working in 14 countries committed to ending hunger. In India it is committed to ignite, kindle and sustain the leadership spirit in women elected to village panchayats.

ISBN: 978-81-7223-9053

2 4 6 8 10 9 7 5 3 1

HarperCollins *Publishers*
A-53, Sector 57, Noida 201301, India
77-85 Fulham Palace Road, London W6 8JB, United Kingdom
Hazelton Lanes, 55 Avenue Road, Suite 2900, Toronto, Ontario M5R 3L2
and 1995 Markham Road, Scarborough, Ontario M1B 5M8, Canada
25 Ryde Road, Pymble, Sydney, NSW 2073, Australia
31 View Road, Glenfield, Auckland 10, New Zealand
10 East 53rd Street, New York NY 10022, USA

Typeset in 10/14 ITC Stone
InoSoft Systems

Printed and bound at
Thomson Press (India) Ltd.

Contents

Preface

This book started out as a project to document the stories of some remarkable women leaders in the panchayat system across the country. Each of them had passed through the trainings organized by The Hunger Project-India. Over the last nine years, The Hunger Project-India and their partners have gone into rural areas across 14 states, to encourage women to participate in the political process, equip them with the knowledge required to perform their roles as panchayat leaders efficiently, and empower them through leadership and skills trainings. Thousands of women pass through these trainings, and each of their stories is unique. Yet in the rush of every day life, these rarely get documented; those that do, get stuck within the confines of reports and documents that do not reach a wide audience.

The project that gave rise to this book, however, aimed at putting out some of these remarkable stories into the public domain. As one writer after another agreed to be part of it, it metamorphosed into an experiment that would take each author from her city to visit one elected woman panchayat president – somewhere called gram pradhan, somewhere sarpanch, elsewhere mukhiya – in her home and village, and help tell her story to the world. In doing so, not only did the sarpanchs get an opportunity to reflect on their lives and narrate their tales, but the writers were also affected by the experience, raising probing and relevant questions and seeing for themselves the odds against which women struggle. It is but a small attempt to bring to light the 'gender capital' that is being built up in the country and the changes at many levels – social, political, personal and structural – that the involvement of women in local governance has unwittingly sparked.

Introduction

When the Best Man for the Job is a Woman

The history of women in politics, in South Asia, is beset with contradictions. Despite having strong women as prime ministers and presidents, it hasn't necessarily translated into any real or radical change in the representation of women and their concerns in mainstream politics. Various reasons are given for this: Women in these top positions have been 'wives, widows and wards' of men in power, and have therefore inherited political seats in line with our feudal, patriarchal traditions and penchant for dynasties. Or, they have played the political game on existing terms with powerful male mentors, doing little to actively carve out a different agenda that looks at the interests of women as a political category. The dominant feeling is that merely having prominent women in politics has little to do with true political empowerment of women. Consistently, the representation of women in higher levels of parliament across the region has been dismal: A meagre 2 per cent in Bangladesh, 8 per cent in India, 5 per cent in Nepal and 4 per cent in Sri Lanka (Ghimire, 2006).

On the other hand, radical changes have been sweeping another level of politics on the ground. The 73rd Constitutional Amendment, which mandated elections be held for membership to the panchayati Raj[1] and reserved one-third of the seats for women in the Panchayat system of local governance in India, has had far-reaching consequences. It has been called a 'silent revolution', 'the greatest social experiment of our time' and 'one of the best innovations in grassroots democracy in the world' (Dugger, 1999). Since it came into effect in 1993, more than three million women have become politically active, with over one million of them being elected to public office every five years. This is a staggering statistic for any nation.

However, like in mainstream politics, here too, popular opinion is shrouded in disenchantment, and is ripe with misgiving. Critics, since the beginning, have panned the 73rd Constitutional Amendment, saying that it is a token process where the real people in power are the husbands of the elected woman representatives. Unravel the discomfort a little more, and other fears come tumbling

[1] Panchayati Raj is a decentralized system of governance in which 'gram panchayats' or village councils are the basic units of administration; it is often called the foundation of the Indian democratic system. It has three levels: village, block and district. At the village level, it is called a panchayat (traditionally meaning an assembly of five [wise] elders acceptable to a village community as a voice of authority) comprising anything between 7 to 31 members. The block-level institution is called the panchayat samiti, while the district-level institution is called the zilla parishad. Different states in the country may have variations in name and in levels.

out. Can women govern at all? That too, 'poor, uneducated, oppressed' women? Do they have the capabilities? What do 'illiterate, ignorant, village women' know about politics? Do they even know what our laws, schemes and development policies are? Aren't they all just puppets, rubber stamps, proxy? Isn't it all eyewash?

Even 15 years after the 73rd Constitutional Amendment, these questions have never quite been satisfactorily answered. And even if they have in some measure, a mid-term appraisal, 'State of the Panchayats 2006-2007' done by the Ministry of Panchayati Raj, shows how women have surpassed their reserved quota, constituting anything from 37 per cent to 54 per cent of panchayat members in different states. An AC Neilsen ORG MARG survey conducted in 2008 across 24 states, evaluating the impact of 10.5 lakh women in Panchayati Raj, highlighted the fact that these women no longer depend on husbands or other men to take all the key decisions (Sehgal, 2008). But so deep are the misgivings, that these findings are still considered to be suspect. It is somehow impossible to convince sceptics – and when it comes to women in politics, everyone is a sceptic – that this is only part of the picture.

These stories of female heads of panchayats across India, are set against the backdrop of this uneasy public perception of women in local governance. Four years after the 73rd Constitutional Amendment was put into action, academic Kumud Sharma observed: 'During the last four years the responses from various sections have ranged from euphoria to apprehension,' and she articulated what had been on the public's mind: 'Is it possible to find one million "suitable" women as candidates?' (Sharma, 1998)

Independent writer and researcher, Indira Maya Ganesh, finds one such 'suitable candidate' in the Kalahandi district of Orissa. Educated, articulate and passionate about the travails of her adivasi community, she was encouraged by them to contest and was elected sarpanch two years ago. Ganesh finds Deepanjali Majhi in a difficult phase, still raw and fresh into her term, the 'euphoria of her victory having nosedived into the cold hard wall of politicking and corruption'. The post-election throes have given way to serious concerns: Deepanjali is disillusioned with the system, tense with the interpersonal minefields that must be tread in local politics, and has just come to terms with the reality that women are always vulnerable in unique ways. Ganesh comes back with other questions: Is there such a thing as a 'suitable candidate'? However educated, politically aware and committed they are, can women ever become anything other than their gender, sexuality, and body? How do we prepare women to be suitable for a field that is masculine, violent and patriarchal in itself, where women can be targeted using the oldest methods in patriarchy's book? 'In the end people will ask... was she dutiful?' says Deepanjali's mother-in-law to Ganesh, putting things in perspective.

One thousand kilometres across the country, poet, dancer, writer Tishani Doshi meets Chinapappa in Pachinakapalli, Tamil Nadu – another first-timer in the panchayat, and in the middle of her term. She has already found some spotlight with her actions to facilitate the education of children from the outcaste Irular tribe. As Doshi witnesses the complex terrain that is rural life, and the multiple layers of oppression that a woman in panchayat has to negotiate, she is overcome with tiredness and 'sapped by the enormity of the task at hand'. 'It seems quite unconquerable,' she writes. The expectations people have of women like Chinapappa and other 'star candidates' are very high, but Doshi asks how our expectations can be the way they are, given the multiple shackles that bind women levelling an unequal playing field. By seeing how things are in reality – in Chinapappa's reality – Doshi is forced to re-assess her own expectations and benchmarks of judgment.

Chinapappa, while struggling in her own way, is lucky to have not yet encountered the other obstacles which come with the post of being president of the panchayat – the police complaints, court cases, a 'no confidence' motion or the application of Section 40, a rule which allows an enquiry to be instituted against any elected representative. Novelist Manju Kapur encounters the nitty gritties of life in politics, as she travels through the heart of the country, to Tighra in Madhya Pradesh. Here she meets Sunita Adivasi, a first-timer whose term is coming to an end, but who has learnt enough about politics for a lifetime in these five years. Sunita is battling Section 40, an onslaught of court cases, and has lived out an incredible trajectory in her one term itself.

Women members of the panchayat suffer many of these problems, but the president or the chairperson's post is particularly vulnerable to these onslaughts, being the hand that signs on the dotted line to release finances. Sharma (1998) has noted that 'Reservation for women as chairpersons is the biggest irritant to many, as it undercuts the power of male aspirants from the landed upper class/

caste, who for generations dominated politics at the local level.' In interviews with 99 women panchayat leaders, the Hunger Project office in Madhya Pradesh found that Section 40 and other tools (such as the Two Child Norm, which declared all candidates with more than two children ineligible to contest local elections) are used routinely to threaten and undermine those candidates who become too effective, thus sabotaging 'business as usual'.

In the case of Maya Bhakhuni, however, it did not take Section 40, but plain old-style elections to thwart her political ambitions. Up in the hills of Uttarakhand, journalist Abhilasha Ojha visits Maya, former sarpanch of Boonga village, on the heels of her loss in the elections. Maya's tenure has sparkled with progress and she has demonstrated that she is an efficient and dedicated sarpanch, yet she loses by 50 votes, a crucial election that would have helped her consolidate the work achieved in her first term. She is under the impression that it was a loss by chance – the other candidate gave bribes and distributed alcohol to buy votes, she alleges – but Ojha wonders if it could be Maya's outspoken nature and aggressive confidence that lost her the seat? Ojha could be right: A study by SUTRA (1995), an NGO in Himachal Pradesh that works on issues of women's political and social empowerment, found that forerunners of women's self-help groups in their area more often than not lost elections because women leaders were seen as a threat; people wanted female candidates who were 'soft', 'docile' and essentially easier to manipulate.

The way the elections played out, also echo concerns brought up repeatedly. Studies of all-women panchayats in Maharashtra (Aalochana, 1995; Datta, 2001) highlight the fundamental problem of elections that are woman-unfriendly: unsafe, undemocratic, criminalized and characterized by strategies 'typical of those institutions that men control', such as free liquor, money and other incentives (mostly for men). Frustrated at being unable to break through this pattern, an activist says pointedly, 'Are we training women to adjust to adversary politics or to change the political scenario?' (Aalochana, 1995). The women panchayat members themselves are faced with confusion regarding their political role and social position. 'They expect us to behave like women and think like men,' they lament.

Maloti Gowalla, however, suffers no such identity crisis; she has learnt how to strike a balance over seven years of experience in different levels of local politics. Writer Sonia Faleiro meets Maloti in the verdant Chamong tea estate of Assam, whose people lead a cocooned existence. With the delicate tread of a ballet dancer, Maloti negotiates a diverse constituency and microcosm that is life within the 'bagaan'. Everyday, development work is kept on its toes, as Maloti rides her bicycle through the estate, making sure that the workmen don't fall asleep during work hours. Maloti feels that women have a different way of governing: they use persuasion and dialogue, rather than coercion and violence. While Faleiro does not validate such a generalization, she admits that Maloti's ways of governing are unique – we get a glimmer of her innovative ideas, persuasion skills, and innate leadership even before she actively entered politics, when she persuaded 12 other women to help her pave a main road going through the tea estate. 'I noticed how bad the road was... and I thought about how difficult it would be for my son to walk or cycle down that road when he was old enough to go to school,' Maloti tells Faleiro.

This is not an unusual refrain. Studies have shown that issues like water, education and roads are uppermost on women's minds (Datta, 2001). If the question is whether increased female representation in panchayat has transformed the political agenda, the answer is yes. Simple things like building a road, public toilets, a boundary wall for a school, a well or street lights – these women seem to have a different stake in furthering a development agenda for their village. After all, like Maloti and the women who helped her, they are personally affected, being the ones who fetch water from afar, face physical risks when going into jungles to relieve themselves, struggle to keep the household running, or take responsibility for their children's well-being and education.

Other questions also come up, on whether women really do anything differently from men. Does women's presence in politics mean better politics? Without resorting to essentialism – it is by now established that female members of the RSS, Shiv Sena or any other politically mobilized women's cohort can do as much damage as their male counterparts (Bacchetta, 2003; Sen, 2008) – let us look at some of the evidence which shows that a dominance of women in the structure does make a positive difference. Studies of all-women panchayats have shown them to be strikingly corruption-free, with the community at large also perceiving them to be non-corrupt (Datta, 2001).

This is something of a rarity in politics, as veteran journalist Kalpana Sharma finds out when she goes to meet

Veena Devi, the mukhiya of Loharpura in Nawada district of Bihar. The state, while being notorious for criminality and corruption, boasts of the highest percentage of women in local governance: 54 per cent of panchayat members are women. Can the rising numbers of women in panchayats make a dent in this environment? Sharma marvels at Veena Devi's transformation from a child bride, to a young widow, to a seasoned politician with aspirations for the parliament. But as she accompanies her to two of her constituent villages and watches how corruption plays out on the ground, she wonders how long Veena Devi can hold out in this quicksand, especially as she ascends to the next level of mainstream politics where things are likely to get even more dirty and dangerous.

If Veena Devi's irrepressible advance is inspiring, the reputation that Kenchamma has earned over the years, is heartening. The editor of the book, Manjima Bhattacharjya traverses coffee plantations and betel nut groves of Chikmagalur in Karnataka, to meet Kenchamma, a witness to how things have changed since she first dramatically entered the Tarikere panchayat as their first Dalit woman president in 1993 soon after the 73rd Constitutional Amendment. Kenchamma did not contest the following term, but returned consequently as president of the panchayat in 2004. Bhattacharjya finds Kenchamma's status has undergone a remarkable change because of her political participation, but her life as such, remains eerily unchanged. She is still the poor Dalit woman overburdened with responsibilities, toiling for daily wages, supporting her family, and also looking after the development needs of the village. But, what has she got in return, asks Bhattacharjya.

Kenchamma continues to live in a leaking, thatched hut, shelling betel nuts with callused hands for daily wages (often foregoing this to carry out her panchayat work) and eking out a hand-to-mouth existence for her entire family, in a community where the caste hierarchy is only minimally bruised. How can political power and social powerlessness co-exist so strikingly?

Kenchamma's story also shows us the kind of scrutiny that women in panchayat must undergo, how much harder the questions are for women. The expectations from women panchayat leaders are inordinately high – from their constituents, from the State which laments its expenditure on this 'social experiment' and that the 'outlays don't match the outcomes'. One wonders who is recording the 'report card' of all the male panchayat members? Who's watching if they are keeping to their word and committing themselves to the cause of development? Are they also doing unpaid, unrewarded work of building an infrastructure for the daily survival of their families and communities?

These are the many questions that linger while we see the bigger picture unfold. As the stories progress from being about the newest in politics to the one with the most experience, from the tentative first years and new concerns of Deepanjali, a woman fresh from the victory of her first election, to seasoned players like Veena Devi who is now well into her second term and making a career of politics for herself, or Kenchamma who has seen the changing face of women in politics since she first stood for elections in 1993 – a mural emerges of the trajectory of women in local politics in India. A trajectory beset by pitfalls and obstacles, but at the same time, illuminated by heartening possibilities and carving into the fabric of Indian society some deep cuts from which there can be no turning back.

Manjima Bhattacharjya
20 May, 2009

A Suitable Candidate

Deepanjali

Indira Maya Ganesh

The Kalahandi of my imagination is a brown, emaciated land. Like many Indians, I hadn't heard of the district till the 1980s, when the nation was shocked by the news report of a famine-struck family who sold their child for food, prompting a visit from the then prime minister, Rajiv Gandhi.

So, what I wasn't expecting was the sight of lush green paddy fields, broken by the pure white of thin-legged herons and mist-wreathed mountains. The natural beauty of Kalahandi felt eerie, considering the horrific violence that had been taking place in the neighbouring district of Kandhmal, a mere hour from the Titlagarh road. Two weeks before, Hindutva-inspired thugs had begun scouring villages, seeking violent revenge for the murder of a Vishwa Hindu Parishad leader, Lakshmananda Saraswati, allegedly committed by Maoists. Lakshmananda's 'cause' had been to prevent the conversion of forest-dwelling tribals to Christianity by setting up educational and health facilities in Hindu ashrams. The fall-out of his death was acts of rape, torture, looting and arson against defenceless adivasi communities.

A blanket of tension envelops the region. But some of this dissipates as we travel to Rupra Road village, in Narla block, to meet a young sarpanch called Deepanjali Majhi. The villages are separated by long, lonely distances marked by deeply cratered and unfinished roads, devoid of any electricity or telephone poles. Rupra Road, a little over an hour's journey from the district headquarters Bhawanipatna, however, is atypical in Kalahandi. It has a considerable population of Sindhi and Marwari businesspeople who deal in the wholesale trade of dals, mustard and nigella seeds. The archaeological site in Asuragarh, nearby, also ensures some visibility and traffic through the area. Having its own metre gauge track means that it is not as remote as many other villages in Kalahandi.

We arrive at the clean-swept Majhi compound at the edge of the village. Deepanjali welcomes us in surprisingly fluent Hindi and immediately busies herself with preparations for chai and snacks. Outside, things are quiet. Her sister-in-law plays with her year old son; her mother-in-law sits on the step looking out at Lanjulguda, the imposing mountain that looms over the Majhi homestead. Across the road, the neighbours tend to their goats, women dry their hair in the sun and children fight and cry. There is nothing remarkable about this slice of rural life, except perhaps that 28-year-old Deepanjali is the first woman president – the sarpanch – of the Rupra Road panchayat.

Inside her cool, low-ceilinged, mud-red home, Deepanjali shows me around. She points to a row of six small brown ceramic teacups in a box on a narrow shelf on her kitchen wall and says, 'I got them as a wedding present, 11 years ago. I will use them today since it is a special day.'

I notice three pairs of freshly polished, sparkling white Bata canvas shoes on a shelf in the main room. They stand out against the red walls. 'Three children?' I ask.

'No, two sons – Aju and Sonu. I got an extra pair for Aju since he is growing so fast. I like to plan ahead,' she replies.

Deepanjali studiously ignores questions about Kandhmal and her work as a sarpanch. 'Later, later... we will walk around the village, then you will understand things here,' she says. Instead, she begins to talk about how she arrived in Rupra Road and the circumstances leading to her election as the sarpanch.

Deepanjali's family is from Bolangir, a district known to be more socio-economically advanced than Kalahandi. Bolangir has been a princely state governed by a line of progressive royalty who promoted forestry, agriculture, social services and education for its people. Women from here are considered to be strong-willed and politically conscious because of their access to education. Deepanjali's father was a Gond tribal, as is her 'elder mother', her father's first wife; her own mother, her father's second wife, was a Kondh. As a result, Deepanjali says, she grew up watching her mother face discrimination and slights from her elder mother's family.

'As a child you see these things and you realize that you never want to be silent again. You want to be able to speak up,' she says simply of what must have been a complex situation. It is a common practice among the tribal communities here to have two such families living together, and Deepanjali was especially close to her elder half-brother and half-sister. Leaving them to attend college in Bhawanipatna was very hard for her, but her father, a mailroom attendant in the postal service, had worked hard to secure the finances for her education and was keen that she acquire an Arts degree. 'My father was everything to me. He made everything possible. I could not let him down,' she says.

Deepanjali had completed two years of her BA degree at Bishwanathpur College in Bhawanipatna. She enjoyed it very much, although it presented many challenges, such as having to walk five kilometres to get there, not being able to afford a bicycle like other girls, nor being able to dress like them. She observes: 'I became aware of social differences between separate groups in our society, but somehow it didn't affect me very much. I was keen to work hard and fulfill my father's dreams.' It was while she was in college that Deepanjali was first approached by 'some local people' to stand for panchayat elections for the Ambatola seat in Rayagada district. For a young adivasi woman to go to college was a rarity in 1997, and that too, one who was not affiliated to any political party. But Deepanjali was unsure, and her family was unwilling to let her contest at so young an age. That part of Rayagada was not safe for a young unmarried woman: there were too many drunks who could create trouble.

Why was she approached? Were the adivasi leaders keen to field fresh, young representatives, or, was it that a young unmarried woman would be easier to manipulate? 'A bit of both maybe,' ponders Deepanjali. 'I cannot deny that I was a good candidate even then. I am an adivasi woman who would speak her mind even as a young person. Maybe I had some kind of reputation.'

It was just before she entered the third year of her degree that there was a proposal for her to wed Rupradhar Majhi, a primary school teacher. It was decided that she would marry and move to Rupra Road.

The public perception that Deepanjali would be a suitable candidate did not wane even after she married and settled into her role as wife and mother. She was well-educated, compared to most women in Kalahandi – articulate, confident, and an adivasi. She was also probably helped along by history, for 25 years ago, Deepanjali's grandfather was a sarpanch from Narla block as well. With these credentials, she was a candidate whom other adivasis would be happy to support. So in 2006, Deepanjali was again approached by a string of local community members to contest in the panchayat elections scheduled for February 2007. One of them was a well-known community elder who offered her financial and political support. 'But,' she confesses, 'in reality he is a bit shady; no one knows how he makes his money.' A friend's father and her own father-in-law cautioned Deepanjali against falling in with this plan and so she declined. 'They thought the man was going to eventually take my seat after having given me money and support. They were probably right,' she says.

By this time Deepanjali was not a young bride anymore; her children were growing up and didn't need her constant attention. She recalls, 'After the children went to school, what was there for me to do? I used to just sit at home. What was the point of going to college if I didn't do anything afterwards? I wanted to do some community work, and so, when the youth groups and women's self-help groups (SHGs) also said that they were behind me, and people from the area wanted an adivasi candidate to represent them, I thought... why not, I can stand for elections. I can be the sarpanch.'

Despite her confidence, there were moments of doubt and hesitation. At first, she wasn't aware that she was eligible to stand from any seat she wanted. It was another woman sarpanch who reassured her that women could stand from the general/adivasi category seat, and were not restricted to the women's category seats alone. 'It was such a breakthrough in my understanding, and few people know this: the 33 per cent reservation does not mean that women can contest *only* from those seats, it just means that men can contest only from 67 per cent of the seats. Ask people here if they know this, and you will find that they do not.'[1]

When Deepanjali decided to contest from the open seat, some members of the opposition paid her a visit to let her know that she should stand from the women's seat only. The seven other men she was standing against were distantly related to either her or her husband, all of them Kondhs as well. The only one she was really scared of, however, was the one who had run for the Legislative Assembly seat in the last elections. He had 'connections', he could be threatening when drunk, and the Majhis found him hanging around their house late at night.

Rupradhar Majhi, a mild-mannered man, was very worried. Says Deepanjali: 'My husband was unhappy with my interest in politics and he continues to be so. He is a little scared of what it will do to our lives. There is violence, there is corruption... He said he did not want any lafda (trouble) – or worse, a police case. But these

[1] Aradhana Nanda of The Hunger Project concurs that this has been one of the most important achievements in their work with women in the area: '... many women used to be unwilling to contest elections when they thought there was no chance of them winning. They have no idea that the laws actually allow them to contest from all seats; instead they think they are restricted to a few reserved seats.'

things are part of political life.' Rupradhar did not know if his wife could handle such tensions. He was sure that he could not. Nor could he stand up to the community that asked why his wife was not staying confined to the limits of the women's category. He did not want to deal with the rumours and questions, the things people whispered amongst each other. Some of them said it out loud. Locals summoned Rupradhar Majhi to talk some sense into him and said: 'Your father used to carry loads of earth on his frail shoulders for your upkeep. Now that you have got an educated wife, who has never ventured out of the four walls, she thinks she can be the sarpanch of the panchayat. Are you not left with an iota of shame?'

Deepanjali's mother-in-law, Tara Majhi, had her opinions too: 'I never thought a woman from our family would become a sarpanch. I suppose things are different from my time. I was very happy to be a wife and take care of my family. But now women are educated, they think they can be more than that.'

Around the time of the nominations, Deepanjali's uncle died. Her husband was nervous about facing the stream of supporters visiting their home every day, so he volunteered to represent the family at the funeral, leaving Deepanjali at home. He told her that she should not let people persuade her. 'He asked me to make people go away and not crowd around our house all the time,' she recalls. But Rupradhar could not avoid the questions and comments, as much as he tried to. 'It was a difficult time for him,' Deepanjali says, straight-faced. If she absorbed her husband's fears, she did not show it, nor did she indulge them. Instead she went about planning for the elections.

Rupradhar Majhi's fears were never really put to rest, but Deepanjali's nomination was in and campaigning had to begin. A total of 3,500 voters and 8 candidates focussed their attention on the Rupra Road panchayat seat. Friends, SHG members, youth and adivasi groups, all rallied around Deepanjali to show their support. Her supporters helped organize visits across the block, to the youth and women's groups, even to remote Dalit villages where adivasis are not welcome. 'I was very relieved to have all this support, but there is a price to pay... maybe not now, but some day, they will want something back,' she observes. For the short-term, however, Deepanjali focussed on winning. She pushed herself to new limits. She recalls:

> I remember going with my supporters to Dendhrobahali, about eight kilometres away. We had to go on foot, up a steep hill. The Congress leader in our area said that I should not take a vehicle. I did not want to seem like a politician anyway. It was very late by the time we arrived and we were all hungry. But then we realized that we had reached a scheduled caste village, and we were adivasis. We were not supposed to eat with them. My group was hot and tired, but I encouraged them to carry on till we got back. I was not sure if even I would make it back without any food or water, but I had to do it to keep the spirits of my group up.

Between canvassing, voting and the announcement of results, in any election across India, there are countless ways to stymie the democratic process. This is when the greatest vigilance is required and Deepanjali's supporters did not fall short. They were well-prepared with their strategies. The biggest village in the block, Balwaspur, has a long tradition of electoral misconduct. When the time came to count the votes, Rupra Road ensured that they did not declare their results till Balwaspur had; that way Balwaspur could not stamp extra ballots to exceed the Rupra Road tally. Her supporters blocked the entrances to homes in Jalguda where rival party supporters were going house-to-house with wads of cash to buy votes in advance. Everything proceeded as expected – even the fights, aggression and drunken brawls between the opposing camps.

The tally began trickling in with one vote from one village, then 3, then 67, and later 500 votes from Rupra Road. Neither Deepanjali nor her campaign managers got much sleep the night before the results were announced. And then the final tally was in: Deepanjali had won with 884 votes, by a margin of 116. Deepanjali Majhi was ready to be the new sarpanch of Rupra Road.

***

Driving through the main street of Rupra Road, Deepanjali begins to open up about her work and experiences as the sarpanch over the past 18 months. The village is bustling and cosmopolitan, judging by the four different styles and weaves of women's saris on display at the market: adivasi, Dalit, Marwari and Oriya. Children yell out, 'Sarpanch, sarpanch...' as our jeep goes by.

'How did you celebrate your win in the election?' I ask.

'Well, nothing much... the usual, like distributing some sweets. But the important thing for me was to start working to improve the village,' she replies.

Deepanjali's no-nonsense, focussed approach is propelled by the struggle to survive. 'I am more concerned with why my community is without water and food, or why children are malnourished,' she says. One of her first tasks was to petition the block administration to sanction tube-wells for her panchayat. Her commitment is to improve the lives of women and children, and enhance livelihood opportunities for the entire community. Deepanjali noticed that women were consistently excluded from government pension and food schemes, but were still willing to involve themselves in community activities. So she urged women to apply for work under the National Rural Employment Guarantee Scheme (NREGS)[2], gave SHGs the priority when local ponds were auctioned for pisciculture, and transferred some Public Distribution System (PDS) responsibilities to SHGs as well. She observes, 'More women are coming forward to work, and to take on responsibilities to support me. This is good because they are hardworking and don't waste time. Now they come forward and demand things from the community, leaders and the administration.' One of Deepanjali's supporters, a local health worker, Deeptimayee, is clearly appreciative:

> Things have improved after Deepanjali has begun her tenure. During previous male sarpanchs' terms, anybody could come here to the health centre and bother us. Drunkards would hang around here, or at the panchayat office, and the women would feel scared to go anywhere. Deepanjali has stopped all this now. In fact, you can

[2] Under this Act, passed in 2005, any adult in a rural area willing to do casual labour at the minimum wage, is entitled to employment on productive public works within 15 days of applying for a job, subject to a limit of 100 days of guaranteed employment per household per year.

see more women coming to the panchayat office than men.'

Khysamanidhi Pradhan from the gram panchayat office says that Deepanjali is a hands-on and involved sarpanch:

> She is confident in using the Right to Information Act and tries to make her panchayat's information more accessible to the public. She gets involved with every day grassroots issues. For example, when people have problems opening their bank or post office accounts under the NREGS, she goes there and helps them out. She takes an interest in PDS distribution and keeps an eye out for trouble there. I have seen her with SHG members while they distribute kerosene to the public.

However, criticism and obstacles also follow on the heels of Deepanjali's achievements. The euphoria of her victory, and her commitment to work, come up against the cold hard wall of politicking and corruption. Deepanjali's emphasis on women's concerns is seen by some sections as playing favourites, especially with the SHGs. The panchayat secretary Dhanurjaya Patel hits out at her:

> Deepanjali has given the PDS distribution work to women's self-help groups. Also, exclusive bidding for the pisciculture ponds was given to the SHGs. She is looking after the demands of women more. If any bank is denying a SHG a loan, then the sarpanch herself goes to the bank and negotiates with them. She loves to work and she loves to make everybody else work.

'They say that I am playing favourites,' says Deepanjali. 'What else will they think when there are so many people

and so little to go around? There are a limited number of ration cards, and too many people who apply for them; there are limited grants for widow pensions, but far too many old women who need them. I have to wait for an old woman to "vacate" her position before I can allocate the next grant,' she laughs at her own black humour.

Things have got worse for Deepanjali ever since most of her campaign supporters began to shift loyalties. Their grouse is that she has not been able to deliver on what she promised them, but for little fault of her own. Of the 50–60 lakh rupees sanctioned to Deepanjali's office, only 10 per cent has actually been received. The hold-up in the transfer of funds can be traced back to other panchayats in the block who have not utilized their existing funds, nor accounted for them. Thus the Department of Rural Development Activities (DRDA) in the block administration has stopped all further disbursements till all the accounts are in order. This delay has upset the youth groups who were keen to get their projects underway – projects that Deepanjali had promised they would be funded for.

The enthusiasm that kept her campaign afloat has waned, and some of her supporters now work with members of the opposition who run liquor breweries and offer contractual work. Now, when she needs the support of the community, it is not forthcoming. Says Deepanjali, 'No one is available to come and help me. They all say "my mobile couldn't be reached because there was no network." Anyone can say that and disconnect the phone and go to sleep while the sarpanch faces the music.'

We have driven through Rupra Road to the other end of the village to visit Premlata Khuntla, Deepanjali's

naib-sarpanch (deputy sarpanch). Premlata's house sits in a clearing in front of a grassy meadow that separates it from the primary school compound. School has just given over and children stream out in twos and threes, the older children in front, the younger ones trailing behind. It is heartening to see girls of all ages emerge from the schoolhouse. For a few moments there is no other sound but the rising pitch of childish after-school chatter. Children gawk and wave at us as they skip past Premlata's house.

I am excited at the thought of not one, but two, women at the helm of Rupra Road. Curiously, however, Premlata is very quiet. She ignores me and busies herself playing with her brother's new infant son. I am further surprised when Deepanjali sits beside her, but they don't exchange a word, nor look at each other. 'She says her husband is not at home,' translates Aradhana of THP, 'so she cannot talk much.' We spend half an hour in desultory conversation, much of it in Oriya; there is so much unsaid that hangs heavy in the air around us. I realize there is something I have not been told and will discover once we leave.

Premlata's rise from ward member to the position of naib-sarpanch reveals another side of local politics that Deepanjali has to contend with. To garner the support and goodwill of members of the community before the elections, Premlata and her husband spent 40,000 rupees to repair the main road running through the village. Now that his wife is the naib-sarpanch, Khuntla wants Deepanjali to use her influence with the Block Development Officer (BDO) to ensure that he is awarded contracts that will allow him to recover his money. Deepanjali refuses to go along, leading to a stiff, uncomfortable stand-off with Premlata.

The two hardly communicate, except for the most basic and essential matters.

The tension in interpersonal relationships, however, is far less than the extent of ethical and moral bankruptcy in the administration. Negotiating this murky world of corruption has implications for a woman like Deepanjali, who wants to be, and be seen as, an effective leader.

The implementation of the NREGS in Rupra Road is one such area of concern, bearing out official reports that Orissa shows some of the worst nation-wide results in the implementation of the scheme.[3] The NREGS is unpopular here precisely because it seeks to eliminate the middle-man and the contractor: the worker is paid directly. Narla Block's former BDO does not want to mobilize people to apply for jobs, and Deepanjali believes that 'he just did not want to do any work.' Jobs under the NREGS are demand-driven, not allocation-driven. If a position does not receive enough applications, it cannot be sanctioned – thus it is responsive to the needs of people. Moreover, what is the need for local administrators to promote a scheme that gives them little to gain through kickbacks? They would rather find other ways for the scheme to work in their favour. So the BDO's office has spread the idea that NREGS jobs are only for Below Poverty Line (BPL) households, and it continues to dissuade people from applying for jobs.

Another government scheme, the Backward Region Grant Fund, is similarly twisted into a shape that fits the

[3] 'NREGS: no let up in graft charges', *The Hindu*, Online Edition, 23 Nov 2007, http://www.hinduonnet.com/2007/11/23/stories/2007112358640100.htm

interests of those in charge. Deepanjali earlier used it to fund electrification work in the village, but it has now been diverted away from panchayat control to that of the block administration. The collector who passed this order, can thus feel more in control and less accountable.

Outside, the clouds darken and gather for another furious assault on Kalahandi, and inside the cramped jeep, Deepanjali begins to loosen up. She switches from Hindi to Oriya, speaking fast and long. Her voice rises and falls while the rain drums steadily; the windscreen wipers squeak and scrape, dutifully monotonous.

There is something in Deepanjali's words that begins to explain her earlier reluctance to talk about being the sarpanch. 'It is one thing to win, but it is a completely different thing to lead. This is the hardest thing I have ever done,' she says.

Deepanjali speaks of being gradually isolated by male members of the panchayat and panchayat samiti, particularly, Dhanurjaya Patel, who occupies a government-appointed position and therefore wields extraordinary power. Deepanjali finds that she is consistently opposed by him in any conflict of opinions. Patel has his own views, and says: 'Male sarpanchs are better as they know how to manage things. Women sarpanchs do not know much. We have to teach them. Sometimes they act smart and overlook guidelines.'

There is something strangely shocking about the familiarity of this. These are precise strategies being employed to discredit Deepanjali: old as the hills, and deeply gendered. Aradhana continues to interpret what Deepanjali says: 'The most difficult thing is that now they are going too far... they are spreading the rumour that she is having an affair with the new BDO, since he listens to her and not them. Her husband too knows that people are talking. *They are saying that she is having an affair...!'* The implications of this latest violation are lodged deep inside Deepanjali. It is the ultimate, albeit predictable, turn of the knife. She is the sarpanch, but also the wife, mother, woman; a body, sex, gender.

The measure of success and failure for a woman is standard and unchanging; as Deepanjali's mother-in-law Tara says, 'In the end people will ask, "Who was her mother-in-law, who was her father-in-law, was she dutiful?"'

This is precisely the issue: What does it mean to be a 'suitable candidate' for the position of sarpanch? What does it mean to be taken seriously as a political entity? The destiny of a woman in politics, in such a deeply patriarchal culture, is written all over her being. Her political fortunes and actions will rarely be delinked from the politics of sexuality – her femininity (or lack thereof), her marital status, what she looks like and how she behaves. Deepanjali's efficiency and effectiveness as a sarpanch, risk being hinged on who she is and not on how she performs, particularly when she attempts to challenge the traditions of governance in Rupra Road.

But Deepanjali constructs her role as sarpanch in terms of her work for her community. There is perhaps a naiveté in how she pegs this to ideas of truth, principles and commitment, when the world around her turns on the fulcrum of realpolitik. I sense that she struggles with this now, having spent 18 months as the sarpanch and realizing that she has to find another way to negotiate her own, and external, moral positions. At some point in our conversation Deepanjali asks exasperatedly, 'Am I supposed to be the sarpanch or am I supposed to deal with corruption?' She sees them as mutually exclusive, when in fact her experience shows that they are not. To be the sarpanch, is to engage with the corruption: to resist and fight it, fall in with it or turn a blind eye to it. The choices are pathetically stark, or there is no choice at all – violence or passivity, corrupt gains or poverty. How does an idealistic person like Deepanjali survive within a system where corruption is the norm and anything else an aberration?

The support of organizations like THP is a reliable constant at this moment in Deepanjali's life. The organization conducts regular meetings with women sarpanchs in the region and gives them space to discuss their issues and concerns. It also keeps in touch with sarpanchs' families, recognizing that the support and reassurance of close relationships are critical to women trying to effect change within complex and traditional social systems.

It is only the beginning of Deepanjali's journey in politics, and I am not sure what she will lose or gain in the process. I am worried for her as she negotiates the next move and looks ahead with exhaustion at the remainder of her term. When a torch of truth is carried through a crowd, some pallus will be scorched.[4] Perhaps Deepanjali did not expect that it would be hers.

[4] Inspired by an old saying from the Russian Revolution. The original saying reads: 'When a torch of truth is carried through a crowd, some beards must be burned'. (Anon)

Small Wonders

Chinapappa

Tishani Doshi

Even before I meet Chinapappa I am intrigued. I do not yet know about the strange circumstances of her marriage, her ardent love for Rajnikanth, or her ability to whistle like a steam engine, but I am still intrigued. There's her name for a start: *Chinna Pappa* – which translated from the Tamil means 'small child' – a slightly incongruous name for a woman of considerable power. And then, there are the scant details of her life and achievements, which have been neatly typed up on a piece of paper and handed to me for the purpose of this assignment.

Age: Uncertain, probably early thirties.
Caste: Dalit.
Notable achievement: Although being illiterate herself, R. Chinapappa, President of Pachikanappalli Gram Panchayat in Krishnagiri District, Tamil Nadu, has helped 21 children from the Irular tribe to enrol in primary schools, marking their beginning of a journey towards a better future.

It is a bright September day when I arrive in the village of Pachikanappalli, Tamil Nadu. I have left my coastal city of Madras at dawn, taken the highway west towards Bangalore, driven past biscuit-brown rocky outcrops and suicidal lorries, to finally arrive in Krishnagiri district. Before heading out, I meet my translator, Lalitha, who also works as a programme officer for the Tamil Nadu office of the Hunger Project. Lalitha knows Chinapappa well. 'She's great,' she tells me. 'You'll like her.'

Lalitha is an NGO dynamo: passionate and indefatigable. She walks fast and talks faster, and has a penchant for acronyms, which come bursting through her conversation like little avalanches: BDOs, MBCs, SCs, BCs, NREGS, PWDs... 'Slow down,' I beg. 'Explain it to me from the beginning.'

'Don't worry about it,' she reassures me. 'You'll figure it out as we go along.'

After lunch, Lalitha and I wash up and set out into 'the field'. No sooner have we taken a diversion off the main highway than the road transforms into a mud path. Temples and roadside shrines spring up like mushrooms, men in checked lungis and outrageous moustaches lounge around in the bright South Indian sun. Luminous rice fields and coconut trees sway sleepily in a lazy breeze. As we drive further into the interior, I realize we are passing the landscape of Chinapappa's adulthood, possibly her childhood too. These chickens and cows, these scratching dogs and children in uniforms, the KRP dam[1] – all these make up the fabric of her every day life. I begin to wonder, as we go further into the village, what it means to piece together the story of someone's life; to position oneself on the floors of their house and presume to ask questions about love, loss, leadership.

[1] The Krishnagiri Reservoir Project was constructed in the 1960s during the rule of Chief Minister Kamraj. It is situated at a distance of 7 km from Krishnagiri.

***

Chinapappa is not what I expected. She is young, vibrant and attractive, wearing a black sari, hair neatly coiled in a bun, sparkly earrings in her ears. She has an air of vulnerability about her, but walks with authority. She greets me by taking both my hands in hers, and then walks us back to her house – a rectangular, peeling structure with beans drying outside the front door. Inside the house, there is one chair, a fan, a small TV, and a shelf with a music system. Many years ago, the walls must have been painted a vibrant turquoise blue. Now they are faded and chipped. A clock dominates the centre of the main wall, and next to it are framed photographs of various gods and a deceased family member. The window grills hold a cluttered assortment of shoes, implements and empty canisters. Hooks on the wall hold shirts, and a washing line tied across one side of the room, has children's clothes draped across it. Jute mats are spread on the floor for us to sit. A baby squirms in a dirty pink cloth cradle hanging from the ceiling. Thirteen people live in this house.

The house is hot. Electricity in the village is erratic. Flies swarm around us in delight. After a while, I stop bothering to swat them away. Midway through the proceedings, a woman in a maroon sari, wearing gigantic black goggles, comes to sit at the door to listen. This is Chinapappa's mother-in-law, who has just had a cataract operation, but is still working at a nearby construction site. 'I've just come to listen for a while,' she says, feeling free to throw in bits of information into the dialogue, as and when she sees fit. Other people come and sit by the door to do the same without announcing their arrival or leave-taking; they disappear as suddenly as they appear.

Chinapappa doesn't know exactly when she was born, but she estimates she is roughly 31 years old. She has five children ranging from the ages of 5 to 13, three daughters followed by two sons: Punithamani, Jayamani, Anjali, Kavin Kumar, and Shiv Surya. With the birth of each of her five children, all delivered on the floors of this house without a single ultrasound or visit to the hospital, her greatest dream for them was this: that they must be educated. 'Why, I can't say,' she says. 'From when I was very young, I always believed this.'

She herself was only educated until class three. All the people in her family have always been coolies, working as daily labourers on construction sites. The childhood she evokes is a Shakuntala-Heidi-esque existence of going off into the forests with her goats, to pick guavas, climb trees and swim in wells. It was a 'jolly' time she says – the most carefree time of her life. Before she reached puberty at 16, she worked as an agricultural coolie, picking flowers for 20 rupees a day. Later, she worked as a construction worker for 15-20 rupees a day. When she was 18 she met C. Ravi, a stone mason, the man who would become her husband.

Chinapappa is a Dalit woman of the Paraiyar caste. The Paraiyars were at one point considered upper caste in Tamil Nadu. The great Tamil poet, Thiruvalluvar, was a Paraiyar too. Parai, in fact, means to speak or tell. In the earliest Tamil literature, the players of drums, and announcement-makers were Paraiyars. But in recent times the position of the Paraiyar has fallen. They mainly work as agricultural labourers, and fall into the bracket of scheduled caste or SC, which in the complicated, web-like food chain of the Indian caste system ranks alongside phytoplankton: numerous, integral for daily life, yet, by and large overlooked.

When you come from the city, as I did, where caste is something that is masked, rather than highlighted, it is slightly unnerving to land in a place where there is no attempt to hide the hypocrisy. The highly intricate system of subjugation that exists in the villages, the prejudices, rules and regulations, all need to be taken into account in any discussion of governance.

Take Chinapappa's case: In any other situation, one would automatically assume that the president of a committee, or the leader of a group, would be at the top of the social pyramid, rather than at the bottom. In her case, because she is of a lower caste than most of her ward members, she is restricted in where she can and cannot meet them. An SC person cannot go to a backward class (BC) person's house, for instance, but the reverse is possible.[2] In the past two and half years, Chinapappa has never eaten a meal with the men in her committee, because

[2] This kind of segregation, while shocking, pales in comparison to other reports of Dalit discrimination in Tamil Nadu. There have been reported instances where Dalits are denied access to roads, their living spaces (always on the outer fringes of the village) are encroached upon by caste Hindus, their access to clean drinking water is nonexistent. At some teashops the two-glass rule applies: one glass for caste Hindus, another for Dalits. In more extreme circumstances, during anti-Dalit riots, their wells (separate from the others in the village) have been poisoned.

they are better educated, of a higher caste, and are, well, men. 'They are like my fathers,' she says, 'I wouldn't sit with them.'

Chinapappa admits to never having had any grand designs on politics. In 2006, the Pachikanappalli district was reserved for a woman SC candidate, and it was her husband who suggested she stand for elections. Before the elections she didn't even know the names of the political parties, and was barely aware of their symbols. She won by 16 votes, even though the other woman, who stood alongside her apparently, went around bribing people to do otherwise.

Chinapappa has spent 30 months in office, and when I find out how the measure of her day pans out, I wonder where she has the time to fit in her panchayat duties – given that the running of the household is more or less entirely shouldered by her. Her day begins early, at 5.30 a.m. First, she must cook for the entire family. Rice, lentils and vegetables are the staple diet, but a few times a week they eat meat, chicken or fish. Then along with her sister-in-law, she cleans the house and gets the children ready for school. The children leave at 8.30 a.m. and walk the one kilometre to school by themselves. On days when Chinapappa attends to panchayat duties (roughly three times a week), she's gone from 9 a.m. to 6 p.m.

One of the first issues Chinapappa dealt with as panchayat president, was the taking of tenders for 96 coconut trees, belonging to her panchayat jurisdiction. Previously, they had always gone to high caste Hindus, but when she came into power she took 10 people along with her for the bidding, and surprised everyone by winning the bid. Six hundred people from other panchayats were present, and they asked what business she had being there. They assaulted one of her men and created a huge hungama, until Chinapappa stepped in and said, if they were going to fight, they better fight her as well. 'Once I start talking no one can stop me,' she laughs. After a historic 12-year break, she managed to regain the tender for Ward 3. It was a moral and economic victory.

The implications of the coconut tender win are manifold: On one hand, by asserting herself so early in her tenure, Chinapappa showed that she was a force to be reckoned with – and certainly no rubber stamp. The other, perhaps more important outcome of the win, has to do with reclamation. By confronting higher caste Hindus, who assume that something is owed to them just because of the arbitrary circumstances of their birth, Chinapappa sent out a strong signal that this kind of behaviour would no longer be tolerated.

What Chinapappa is most proud of, though, and what she is most famous for in her village, is her work with the Irulars. The Irulars are tribal people, traditionally snake catchers and nomads. They exist beyond the iron-grid fringes of the caste system, in a no-man's-land of their own. One community of Irulars had settled near the KRP dam and were being chased away by the local people time and time again. Finally, the district collector called Chinapappa and asked her if she'd mind if they settled themselves a distance away from the village. Chinapappa not only ensured that they got land in their names and a government grant so that they could build houses for themselves, she also made sure their children were enrolled in school, and provided them with uniforms, school supplies and footwear from her own funds. She organized the installation of a solar lamp so that the children could study at night, and made sure hand pumps were installed nearby so that girls wouldn't be made to fetch water at the cost of their education.

Later in the day, we walk over to visit the children in school. The classrooms are small but bright, children sit on the floor, colourful paintings are strung along the walls, and bags are neatly lined up outside. GOOD AFTERNOON MISS, they shout, shooting up on their feet, hands at salute on their foreheads. The teacher in charge makes the Irular children stand separately from the others, so we can identify them. 'Let the new children who live across the road come to the front of the class,' she instructs. A ragged bunch of children, markedly poorer than the rest, with runny noses and large, malnourished eyes, uniforms hanging off their shoulders, huddle towards the front door. One of them is wearing what used to be a glitzy party dress, but is now a mangled, sad piece of tinsel drooping over her scrawny frame.

'They are very sweet-natured,' the teacher tells me. 'They work hard, and so far we've had only one drop out. And as for this one,' she says, pointing to the tallest boy of the lot, 'because of the way they live, it's very difficult for them to give attendance. Only when he's visiting his *chitti,* his father's sister, can he come to school, because his parents live elsewhere, so when he's with them, he's gone for months at a time. But they are obedient and good, and learning well,' she insists, smiling in a benevolent, ingratiating kind of way.

As we make our way back to Chinapappa's house, we discuss her goals for the rest of her term in office: to construct a community hall that can be used for marriage ceremonies, to build a library in the centre of town, to get the defunct hospital working again, to improve sewage and garbage disposal, and most importantly, to negotiate a proper and efficient water supply for the village. The issue of a clean and plentiful water supply is the biggest worry for the village.

While she feels she has fulfilled 70 per cent of her goals, and has two more years to prove her worth, Chinapappa says she feels let down by people who stood by her originally. 'Initially, they were with me,' she says, wistfully, 'but now, they accuse me of all sorts of things, and they want me to do favours for them with contracts and tenders. I can't do that. I'm going to go along with the rules. I don't know when they'll look at me like a sister, when they'll praise me.'

As we get back to her house, her *veetakar* – literally house-owner, or husband – is waiting. He has been dropping in and out throughout the day, occasionally saying something, but more or less keeping a silence. Chinapappa tells him to cut some tender coconuts for us to drink, which he does dutifully. The water is sweet and restoring.

'Ours was a love marriage,' she tells me proudly, and quite firmly.

The circumstances of Chinapappa's marriage sound a little vague. It has to do with the dead relative on the wall. The photograph is of a young woman – her cheeks highlighted to give her an extra blush, her hair plaited and ribboned. There is a garland of fake flowers around her picture. This woman was Ravi's first wife, and also his niece.[3]

[3] The practice of a man marrying his sister's daughter is common in South India.

As fate would have it, Ravi fell in love with Chinapappa at approximately the same time as the niece developed a defective heart condition. The niece, Chinapappa informs us, was brilliant, and training to be a police officer, but as her condition worsened, she was unable to do much, except lie in bed wheezing all day. The mother-in-law is supposed to have said, 'What good is she? She can't even lift a hand to do any housework, better to arrange a second marriage.' This is when Ravi disclosed that he had already found someone he was interested in marrying – a woman who was sturdy, strong, and in good health.

At this point, Chinapappa tells us, she was already pregnant with their first child. The sequence of events that followed involved Chinapappa staying in her parent's house for the duration of her pregnancy and then moving to her husband's house while the first wife was still alive. A few months later, the niece died, making way for Chinapappa to become the rightful daughter-in-law of the house and resident of the village that she would later preside over.

Something of the first wife must have rubbed off on Chinapappa though, because she says if she wasn't involved in politics as a panchayat she would have liked to become a police officer. Chinapappa has a very strong sense of right and wrong. If you ask her what the greatest problem in the village is, she will say it is the men. It might sound sadomasochistic, but the main thrust of her wanting to become a police officer is the ability she'd have to punish men – actual physical punishment. She believes that violence can only be met with violence. What she really hates about men is when they have 'illicit' relationships with other women, and then come home to beat their wives. 'Even my father did this,' she says. 'He was quite a drunkard and he used to beat my mother all the time. But when I came of age, I hit him back one day, and he never raised a hand against my mother again.'

Chinapappa tells a story of a neighbour who used to work as a painter, and who for many years, had relationships with other women and ritually beat the hell out of his wife. Chinapappa finally convinced the wife to file a complaint with the women's police cell, who dutifully picked him up from the house, thrashed him and sent him home. 'The only way to convert them is to beat them into submission,' she insists. 'We need to have a proper domestic lifestyle... Even my husband is not 100 per cent perfect,' she says, trailing off, leaving me to make what I will of that.

Before breaking for the day, I tell Chinapappa I'd like to take a family photograph. For the next hour there is utter confusion. The children who have come home in dribs and drabs are rounded up and quartered in front of the mirror, to be creamed and combed into submission. Chinapappa washes their faces, changes their clothes, adjusts their ribbons, draws kajal into their eyebrows and pottus on their foreheads. She attends to herself as well – heavily smearing some kind of cream onto her nut-brown skin. Only the husband desists from such activity. He stands outside in his lungi, full-sleeved shirt and shiny gold watch, talking on his mobile phone. After much back and forthing, I manage to get the entire family – Chinapappa, husband and five children, to stand outside the front door. None of them smiles. They look as if they're at a funeral. After many jokes cracked from the sideline, Lalitha manages to loosen them up. I capture tiny hints of smiles.

***

The next day, Lalitha and I have only a few hours before we have to leave on our separate ways. We decide to talk to some of Chinapappa's ward members and to generally walk about the village. The first person we meet is Sheila, a feisty 29-year-old woman, who has three children and is training to be a yoga instructor and a beautician. Her house is in the BC area of the village. The walls are freshly painted, the vessels are neatly stacked. Sheila is an instantly likeable and chatty individual. The minute she sits down with us, she begins to talk of her disillusionment with politics. 'I thought I could do something,' she says. 'I sometimes wonder why I stood for elections. No one wants to help. All the men here believe that women have no place in politics, so how will we ever do anything if they keep putting us down?' In the beginning, Sheila says she was very enthusiastic, but increasingly, she feels she gets no help or support from her other ward members, and most of the time, if she tries to raise questions, people are telling her to stop interfering. When we ask her how Chinapappa has been as the panchayat president, she immediately throws up her guard.

'She has done well with the Irulars,' she says, diplomatically.

Sheila and Chinapappa used to be great friends, but now, for some reason, there is a distance between them. 'I don't know what happened,' she says, 'but if I see her on the bus or pass by her at the tea stand, she doesn't even make eye contact with me.'

Just when it appears in our conversation that Sheila is ready to give up a life of politics, in lieu of becoming a beautician, I ask whether she'd accept the top job if it were handed to her. 'Oh yes,' she gushes, 'I know I would do a super job.'

Later that afternoon, we walk through the village talking to random people – school teachers, shopkeepers, a Muslim leader. Most people seem very content with what Chinapappa has achieved. A few criticisms are made about her husband's involvement with the political and business side of things, but the general consensus is that she had made good progress on certain fronts, specifically education, and there every hope that she will work towards rectifying things that the village requires in the remainder of her tenure.

Finally, we make our way to the panchayat office. With us are a few scattered members of Chinapappa's ward, including the clerk, a man called Narasimhan, who has held this position for 16 years. The office is an L-shaped room with wooden shutters, a desk, and a stack of plastic chairs. In one corner there are pickaxes and shovels, and in another a brand new LCD Acer computer and printer lying under a plastic sheet. The Government of India sees fit to supply free computers to every panchayat in the country, without wondering how many of them can actually be used. In the village of Pachinakappalli, there is not a single person with the requisite computer skills to do anything with this piece of equipment. And even if someone took the initiative to learn the skills, there would still be the frequent power cuts to contend with.

As we sit in that room, the overwhelming feeling I have is of tiredness. For two days I have been immersed in the story of this village, its people, its leader. I have heard all the usual complaints – that it is the man behind the woman and the hints at corruption – Chinapappa's husband being a stone mason, *isn't it convenient that he gets all the tenders?*... I have seen pictures of the gram sabha meetings with Chinapappa's husband sitting next to the clerk taking down minutes. But I also know that Chinapappa is not just some rubber stamp who signs where she has to and does what she's told. I know she has fire and her own initiative. I am just sapped by the enormity of the task at hand. It seems quite unconquerable.

Lalitha suffers no such fatigue. She is heckling everyone in the room, taking the discussion into her own hands. I lay my notepad down to rest and put my camera away in its case. For now, I just want to listen. I don't want to hear a translation, for fear that the break will stop the flow in conversation. I will pick up bits and pieces as I can.

Lalitha brings up the subject of water, which Chinapappa had mentioned earlier, as being one of their biggest problems in the village. This is another great irony. Pachinakappalli is situated right next to the KRP dam, but they have no access to the water. 'You can't just complain about it,' Lalitha tells Chinapappa. 'Your job is to draw up a plan, measure the pipes, figure out exactly how much water you need, and how many people it will benefit. You need proper facts and figures, make a pukka plan and present it at the next gram sabha meeting in such a way that they can't refuse you.'

Numbers aren't Chinapappa's forte. Being uneducated, she has a natural resistance to mathematics. When Lalitha asks her how much money she has for disposal in her panchayat, she draws a blank. 'It will be in the records,' Chinapappa says.

Narasimhan the clerk pipes in, 'Six lakhs.' He then proceeds to give a detailed account of how much of that amount has already been spent, and how much more has been earmarked for future projects.

'You must know these things,' Lalitha berates. 'And you,' she tells Sheila. 'You *all* have the right to inspect these books any time you want. Don't you understand?'

On our way back to Chinapappa's house, before our final goodbyes, Lalitha walks alongside me. 'It's very sad,' she says, 'they just don't have the access, the knowledge. How can she be in this position and not know anything about the money? This is the problem, at the end of the day, they still leave the big decisions to men.'

Lalitha has worked with many of the women of this area through various training and empowerment projects. The problem with reservation, Lalitha tells me, is that organized pressure to elect women into positions of power has not necessarily led to a society willing to accept women as political entities. Despite the fact that there are many women in positions of power at the state and central government levels in the country (in the state of Tamil Nadu itself, Jayalalitha has served twice as chief minister), it does not seem to have translated into a ready acceptance at the rural level. Traditional roles of housewives and age-old expectations of womanly submission has led to a somewhat alarming syndrome called pati-sarpanch, where it is in fact the husband of the woman elected, who actually controls affairs. In parts of Tamil Nadu, there have also been allegations where certain Dalit women panchayats have been auctioned off to the highest bidder. The 'auctioned' panchayat's role then, is to literally serve as a rubber stamp to the person who has bought her! In the face of such corruption, Lalitha says, women still have a lot to overcome within the Panchayati Raj system: the weight of bureaucracy, the restriction of mobility and non-literacy-based dependency, to name just a few.

The fact that Chinapappa didn't turn out to be the absolute shining star I hoped she would be, is not so much a disappointment for me, but a stark reality. How can she be anything else? How can she be expected to have any grasp of numbers as large and abstract as six lakhs, when she has only studied till class three, and the combined income of her household of 13 is 10,000 rupees? When you think about all the things that shackle her – her gender, her caste, her lack of education, it is remarkable that she has done what she has. For me, the real story has been the relationship between women like Lalitha, Chinapappa and Sheila – the sharing of knowledge and skills, which must necessarily travel in two directions.

As we walk out to the car to say goodbye, Chinapappa takes hold of my arm; in her other hand, she clutches a purse that says *Burberry London*. 'Come back and see us,' she says. 'And next time, you must eat with us.'

As the car turns off on the highway, I see Chinapappa walking back to her house, carrying all the burden of her responsibilities on her strong, young shoulders. This is the lasting image I take with me. A woman of the new millennium taking charge of her future. A woman who broke social taboos by choosing the man she married. A woman who raised her hand against her father in order to protect her mother. But more importantly, a woman who believes in a different future for her children and for the children of an outcaste tribe. There is no story more modern than this in India. Who says change isn't on the way?

Sarpanch Sahib

Sunita

Manju Kapur

In January 2004, for the third time since the 73rd Constitutional Amendment, the village of Tighra, block Simariya, district Rewa, Madhya Pradesh is going to the polls. Quota decrees that it is the turn of a woman adivasi to be elected sarpanch.

Tighra village is predominantly Brahmin, 100-125 households, as compared to 40-50 adivasi and OBC (other backward classes) combined. Brahmins are the main employers, as well as the main land owners, holding every field the eye can see. These fields are worked by the other castes. Their wages range between 30-40 rupees a day, payable after months, when the sum is further reduced through quarrels over the number of hours worked and the number of days put in.

However, much of that has changed now. Sunita, the elected women representative (EWR) I am interviewing, describes the difference:

> People say our sarpanch is giving us 85 rupees under the National Rural Employment Generation Scheme (NREGS), why should we work for you for less? We are not your servants. For the past three-four years, even when we work in their fields we have nothing to do with them because we work on *adhiya*: a system by which we hire the land, split the costs of seeds, fertilizer, and pesticides. The produce is also halved. We take our

portion directly from the fields. Before, we had to go to the landlords' houses and beg for our share.

Shibani Sharma, programme officer of the Hunger Project in Madhya Pradesh, and I are sitting in Sunita's section of the family complex: mud huts built around an angan. Her two rooms are dark and cool. The cooking space is in front, a sleeping cum storage area at the back. A narrow charpai lies in one corner, in the other, massive mud urns used for storing grain grow from the floor. Openings close to the ground are plugged with wads of cloth, stone slabs rest on top. A small TV is perched on a mud counter, above it a lone dim bulb lights both rooms. A mouse leaps from some hidden place and brushes past my knee.

We are first served sweet, deliciously spiced tea, then rice, dal, mixed sabzi, along with tomatoes and radishes straight from the field. Sunita is helped by her sister-in-law, a thin, soundless woman, with her palla pulled down till her nose. With some persuasion from Sunita, she whispers her name: Suniteri. Her two children, on holiday from school (the former prime minister V.P. Singh has passed away that day) loll about on the mud floor staring fixedly at us.

I marvel at the difference between Sunita and Suniteri. Suniteri is like the other women I see, faces covered, indistinguishable from each other; while Sunita stands out, with her air of health, clear skin and substantial body. She is attractive, laughs often, showing strong, even white teeth. Her blue *bindi* and glass bangles match the flowers spattered against the yellow background of her nylon sari. Tattoos run across the backs of her hands, her nail polish is a fresh bright red. 'Before I became sarpanch I too, could not say anything, like her,' she says, indicating

Suniteri. 'Now I can speak. Now fighting-fighting I have put on weight.'

Lunch over, we tour the village, followed by a line of children – us the outsiders, then the gigglers. The village is a picturesque one, surrounded by fields, with a few hills in the distance. Its houses are neat, either mud huts or small whitewashed brick structures belonging to the Brahmins, set among creepers and bushes. In many doorways I can see the interwoven dark and light rangoli patterns that were visible in Sunita's angan. The unpleasant features are the heaps of trash; plastic bags billowing on piles of hay; Pan Parag packets thrown by the side of the path; tattered, empty, garishly coloured packets of soap which have come to rest on decaying piles of leaves and cow dung pats.

As she takes us around, Sunita points to the hand pumps she has had installed, and to the road she has had paved in the Brahmin section. She proudly leads us to a broad open well, dug for when the pumps run dry. A board next to it proclaims the construction cost to be 1,80,000 rupees. A newly-built platform near the school functions as a meeting place.

I glance at my notes, where her achievements are listed: 25 sanitation points installed, 12 hand pumps repaired, 100 foot capacity pumps created under the Jal Abishek Programme, the construction of roads, deepening of the village pond, and 288 job cards issued under the NREGS. I am duly impressed and ask Sunita if she can come to Satna tomorrow, where we can continue talking without an audience. She agrees readily. Shibani asks her husband for the token permission, but the good humour that follows makes it clear that Sunita needs neither the permission nor an escort.

***

The next day, in our hotel room, she begins her story – a story that started when she was twenty-two. It was the turn of a woman adivasi to be elected sarpanch and Ramesh, a Brahmin, suggested to the adivasi who worked his fields that he put his wife up as a candidate. The Brahmin assured the adivasi elder that there was nothing to be afraid of. Once we make her win, all the work will be taken care of by us, she will just have to sign, he assured.

The adivasi brought this news home. Sunita, his daughter-in-law, had a better suggestion. Her mother-in-law could not travel anywhere, she had a tendency to vomit in a vehicle – wouldn't it be better if she stood for this office instead? This daughter-in-law, still childless, had studied till class five, been married at 10, and had been living in Tighra for the past 13 years. Before the election, she worked with other family members as a labourer, carrying grain or building materials on her head.

The adivasi had only two women in his immediate family, so he agreed. The relatively small adivasi population, rivalries among the Brahmins, and the desire to manipulate the future sarpanch, meant that the opponent persuaded to stand against Sunita was also a relative.

Sunita canvassed by going door to door, pleading for votes through the ghunghat that covered her face, prostrating herself as a mark of respect wherever necessary. On the day of the elections, violence broke out with a brother-in-law beaten up at the voting booth. Sunita won her election by three votes in a counting that was done three times. The village band played through the streets.

Her parents rang Ramesh's son's mobile for news. Yes, Sunita had won, they were told. The laws of pollution meant that no one from Sunita's family could touch the Brahmin's mobile phone.

The trials of Sunita's sarpanchship started immediately afterwards. She had to give a joining letter to the panchayat secretary. A secretary is vital to the sarpanch: their combined signatures are needed to open an account and to withdraw development funds. Development funds are considerable (in four years Sunita has spent over 10 lakh rupees) and their control is behind the bitter and continuous battles she has fought. Unlike the sarpanch, however, who is elected by the village, the secretary is appointed by either the government or the panchayat, on the basis of his educational qualifications. During the tenure of Sahu, the previous sarpanch, there had been three secretaries, appointed and dismissed in order to gain greater financial control. Using the excuse that he wanted a government rather than a panchayat appointee, Sahu got rid of the existing secretary, Santosh Kumar Tiwari. The collector appointed Deen Dayal to the post, but Sahu, outmanoeuvering him, used his nephew Sandip instead. Eventually these three banded together – Sahu, Deen Dayal and Sandip.

Once she had won, Sandip came every day to her house, saying, 'Sarpanch sahib, let's open an account, let's start doing the work.' But Sandip had a bad reputation. It was he who had been behind the violence during the elections. Furthermore, in a culture used to bribery and corruption, he was noted for his money-making sins. Sunita was afraid she would be held responsible, should any irregularities come to light. 'Before we do business, show me the order that says you are the panchayat secretary,' she told Sandip.

Santosh had meanwhile filed a case challenging his ouster, while Sandip filed an application stating that he was the secretary. This was the situation, and Sunita was justifiably wary. She went to Simariya, to the collector. On opening the Tighra file he only saw Deen Dayal and Santosh's name. The collector declared Santosh to be the secretary. Sunita gave her joining letter to him, but the CEO (the state service commissioners who head both the intermediary panchayat and the zilla panchayat are known as CEOs), the man responsible for opening the panchayat account in the joint names of the sarpanch and the secretary, had been bribed by Sandip, and Sunita waited in vain for her account to be opened.

The president of the Janpad panchayat asked for 20,000 rupees before he would help; the administrative officer of the block panchayat asked for 10,000 rupees. Each step of the way, money was demanded, and each time she said the same thing: 'I have no money.' Eventually her reputation would centre around this. 'Everybody gets irritated with me,' she remarked, giggling. 'People say I get my work done, but I don't give any money.'

Months passed and the village account was still not opened. Nearby sarpanchs were proceeding with government-sponsored programmes, but all was quiet in Tighra. No account, no money deposited, no work, no salaries. People began taunting her, now you have a secretary, but still you are doing nothing. After four months of this stalemate, Sunita asked a neighbour for advice – a man who had been sarpanch for 20 years.

'Write an application,' he said. At that time she had no idea what this meant, though in the succeeding years she would become proficient in knowing when they were required, how to go about writing them, processing them, submitting them in duplicate/triplicate, and finally how often to repeat the whole process. But for now, she had to be initiated. In Simariya, her application was written, photocopied and filed with a receipt. Ten days later, when she didn't get a reply, she filed the application again.

Sunita saw Sandip's hand in these delays, his influence and his money, but there was nothing she could do. Back in the village, the questions continued: Why aren't you creating job opportunities? The livelihood of many in the village depended on government-funded work, which was routed through the sarpanch. Without this, the villagers often had to look for employment elsewhere.

Sunita returned to the collector, saying, the CEO is not opening my account. The CEO retaliated with a lie, she doesn't come, what can I do?

The Hunger Project had a programme to facilitate the work of EWRs, and in this connection Sunita was called to Jabalpur, going on a big train for the first time in her life. There she met other sarpanchs who raised their voices in her support: 'Our sarpanch bhai should not be harassed like this.' Encouraged, she returned home, expecting something to happen. But 10 days later still nothing surfaced. Santosh suggested, 'Let's go to Rewa, to the zilla panchayat.' There, they wrote an application to the CEO's boss – our account is not being opened.

Still no action.

The arm of the local big man has a long reach.

The Hunger Project held a subsequent meeting at Sirmore. The CEO was called, ostensibly as a resource person, but actually to make known that the able and the educated were part of the scene as well. Sunita was encouraged to argue her case in front of him. Speak, and speak openly. Tell him everything.

On 30 September, 2006, one year and nine months after the elections, the panchayat account was opened.

Now she had an account, now work could start. Ramesh sent an emissary to Sunita's father-in-law, saying, get her to sign for 5,000 rupees, we need to get a TS from the engineer for a pucca road through the village. (The TS is an estimate that projects the cost of a work in all its detail.) It would be more suitable, said Ramesh, that he arrange for this, somebody was bound to trick his daughter-in-law, who was she but an ignorant, unexposed adivasi woman?

The father-in-law agreed with this assessment. The world was not open to the likes of him, how much less for a young female member of his family?

'In the beginning,' said Sunita, 'I did not talk so much. I went along with everything my father-in-law said.'

The 5,000 rupees was signed for.

The next day the pundit came for another 5,000 rupees.

This too was signed for.

The third day he came for 5,000 more.

At this point, Sunita objected. She may have been inexperienced, but even she knew that 15,000 rupees was not required for a TS. The pundit was outraged. Look at what your daughter-in-law is saying, he told the father-in-law. Has she ever worked outside the home that she knows how much money it takes for a TS? She is always veiled, what does she know about anything?

These questions were repeated to her. Why are you doubting the Brahmin? What do you know? Have you ever left the village? Have you ever seen so much money?

But, said Sunita, if she never met any officer, how would she know what being a sarpanch was all about? She would like to go with the pundit next time for the TS.

Go yourself, taunted Ramesh, through the father-in-law.

All right then, she said, I will go myself. If Ramesh doesn't come, does that mean I can do nothing? Her mother-in-law pounced on her – are you Ramesh's grandmother, that you take his name? But Sunita was learning to go beyond the hierarchies that her adivasi community had been so used to.

She consulted Santosh, who advised her to go to Rewa, the district headquarters. At the office, she asked for the engineer responsible for Tighra. Had he received the 10,000 rupees she had sent? Unsurprisingly, the answer was no.

How much money does it take for a project estimate?

He said, for now nothing. Start work on the pucca road, when I come for the evaluation give me money for both together. (The engineer's cut is standard: 5 per cent for making a TS, 3 per cent for a completion certificate.)

Now Section 40 entered Sunita's life.

Briefly, Section 40 allows an inquiry to be instituted against an elected representative in the case of misconduct or gross negligence. Anybody can do this, a visiting sub divisional magistrate (SDM), the collector, the panchayat department or a member of the gram sabha. During the course of interviewing 99 EWRs, Shibani saw how much it can be used to threaten and intimidate the socially weak. How is it democratic, she demanded, in full possession of her heart-rending facts, to allow the bureaucracy to interfere with an elected representative? Why not allow the panchayat scope to exercise its powers in dealing with irregularities?

When sarpanchs have the authority to distribute money as Sunita does, passions run particularly high. The NREGS scheme particularly lends itself to misuse. Either false attendance sheets are filled to pocket the money, or false attendance sheets are alleged to harass sarpanchs, or pressure is put on the EWRs to fudge figures to make the interested parties happy.

The harassment that flows from Section 40 begins the moment the complaint is made. Repeated court appearances, daily wages lost, long distances to be travelled, bus tickets to be bought, lawyers to be paid, bribing to be contended with, and the staying power of the rich means that this legal tangle is especially hard on the marginalized, poor, non literate and easily frightened. An upper caste man or an arrogant bureaucrat can demand with impunity and they do so. Give me X amount or I will slap Section 40 against you. One SDM filed cases against 29 sarpanchs in 20 days.

Three months after the road was started, Ramesh, along with two other Brahmins, complained to the SDM about the Tighra sarpanch invoking Section 40. The first time the notice came, Sunita was not at home. The Brahmins made sure that the records indicated that she had refused to take it. The second time around, a show cause notice was delivered. By now her family was convinced she was on her way to jail. Her father-in-law said, 'See what happens when you keep doing what you like. This is government work of which you understand nothing. If you had stayed with Ramesh, none of this would have transpired.'

To which she replied, 'If I go to jail, don't visit me. I will be the one to go, not you. Has the warrant come for me or you? Let me think.'

She called her secretary and asked him to read out the notice. His advice was, 'Don't accept it, you can take it next time.'

But she took it, despite everyone's objections.

The next day Sunita set out for Simariya where she met the sarpanch who had helped her earlier. She would have to get a lawyer, he said – she would have to draft a reply. In Simariya, Sunita met the lawyer she had once seen in her house – a pundit who had had some work with her father-in-law. She hired him and her reply was given in the stipulated seven days.

What followed was a battle waged through the courts, through SDMs, collectors, complaints, applications, allegations, counter-allegations, bribes, and threats. Being pressed to take action, the SDM made inspection visits to her village twice. Workers were questioned, their salaries checked. A visiting minister, hearing of her blackened name, accused her: 'Sarpanch sahib, you have swallowed the funds, fudged the figures.'

When she started the well, an application was filed accusing her of using lime instead of cement. Another application was filed, alleging that she hadn't put the mandatory board up, which displayed the total cost of the well project. For a road that cost 6 lakh rupees, they got an engineer to say it was worth only 12,000 rupees.

In the time of Sunita's sarpanchship, the two SDMs and two collectors who refused to take action against her have been transferred. Her attendance sheets with work totalling 3 lakh rupees have been stolen from the audit office. Afraid of the consequences, she has had to make more trips to Sirmore, and file applications in the thana, the zilla and the audit office. Till today they have not been recovered. She has eventually managed to get a duplicate computer copy by giving 100 rupees to a technician.

Sunita has been called to court at least eight times a month to answer one application after another. When they cursed and swore against her, threatened to tear her file, and that too in front of the lawyers, she reported them to the police. They threatened to boycott the mid-day meal cooked by lower caste women for school children. At first, these women were intimidated, but Sunita had the backing of a government programme behind her. Food continues to be made by 'low caste' hands, and all children now eat these meals.

Sunita won a public victory the day an SDM came at five in the evening, in his red light car, demanding to see her records, her attendance sheets, to know what wages she was paying, and to how many. Her attendance sheets had gone to the audit office. As she dealt with his suspicions, she said, 'Sir, I am an adivasi woman sarpanch for the first time. These are Brahmins who say: give a project estimate for 20,000 rupees, out of that spend 10,000 rupees on the work, the other 10,000 rupees give to the engineer, the CEO, the secretary and to us. Because I don't do this, they are against me. Till today the village panchayat office has a lock, the previous records are not available. Officers listen to the Brahmins, they do not understand what is true and what is false.'

'Sarpanch, what are you saying?' came the response.

'You say the sarpanch is a thief – you believe the applications makers – please go and see the well, see how deep it is. Talk to the labourers.'

The SDM went to the labourers. 'How often does she pay you?' he asked.

'In eight to fifteen days,' he was told.

'How much does she pay you?'

'Sixty-five rupees.'

He went to the Sarpanch Bhavan and called the previous sarpanch.

'Why is this building still locked?'

No answer.

'Where are the keys?'

'Lost.'

The SDM got a panchnama (agreement) made, got everybody to sign, then broke the lock and asked Sunita to put her own on the door.

Subsequently, the SDM was transferred.

Sunita's enemies have told her father-in-law, 'When she goes to Sirmore, we will run over her with the wheels of our car. We are Brahmins. Ten to fifteen murders are forgiven for us.'

This was repeated to her. A few days later, after the flag hoisting ceremony on Republic Day, she told a passing relative of Ramesh, through the sari that covered her face, 'You may be forgiven 10 murders, but know that we are forgiven 20.'

The pundit was appalled, 'What are you saying?'

What was she saying? repeated Sunita. They had threatened to run over her, to kill her. If they dared touch her, she would report them.

'If you have become sarpanch, will you murder everyone?'

'I have not murdered anyone, but if there is a sword in my hand, I will use it.'

'We have made you sarpanch, and this is how you behave?'

'You have not made me sarpanch, it was the adivasi female quota and my fortune.'

Passers-by chimed in, saying, 'It's all right, no need to fight.'

'It's not all right. You want that we should remain your slaves. But now know that if you make one application against me, I will make two against you.'

For the next five months, village work came to a standstill. Again the harassment involved her secretary. The Janpad asked her to donate 5,000 rupees towards a jagran, a public religious recital. She objected, 'There are 103 panchayats, if you take money from all, that will be 5,15,000 rupees. So much...! What future blessings can you accumulate if you take money like this?' Soon after, the CEO and the Janpad suspended her secretary. They told her Deen Dayal was her new secretary, but she refused to give him a joining letter. She wrote an application to the Janpad, zilla panchayat and the collector...

And so it goes on.

As our meeting draws to a close, Sunita reflects:

> I have experienced a lot, but I have gone on fighting. Now I think – there was no politician in our family – we

> never knew how to speak for ourselves. But now I can talk, I am not afraid. I tell the pundits – you trouble us a lot. You only want that we should press your feet and not do anything, you want that our children not study and that we do not progress. I tell my family, you are not to go to Ramesh's house, you are not to work with him. Now they do not go. They even say, give us the signal and we will beat him up. I say no, no, there is no need for that.

'Are you glad your term is coming to end? Would you do this again, Sunita?' I ask after listening to her bewildering story that includes almost every member of the political and bureaucratic hierarchy in Panchayati Raj.

'Absolutely.'

I look at her as she sits in front of me, bright, self-assured, with a clear understanding of her rights, imbued with a sense of entitlement. At the entrance of her village is a large pink gateway that proclaims in arching black letters, 'Sunita Adivasi, Sarpanch, welcomes you to Tighra Panchayat,' her name and that of her village inextricably and openly linked.

She was only 22 when she saw an opportunity and grabbed it. Over four years she has made it into just that: an opportunity to change herself, her circumstances and her community's status. Now she is looked upon with respect. Her family supports her instead of criticizing her. She has travelled to Delhi to meet the President of the Congress Party, Sonia Gandhi, whom she had the courage to accost with an unscheduled question, 'Didi, please listen to the problems from Madhya Pradesh, listen to the ways in which we are harassed by Section 40.'

Through the fighting, the power struggles, the bribes, corruption, threats and hundreds of applications, she has been exposed to the world and grown both in confidence and experience. Already she is looking to the time when her tenure will be over – to further political possibilities that being a sarpanch have opened to her. Her political exposure has meant that she can never go back to being the veiled, fire tending, wholly domestic creature she once was. She has a public life and she will not give it up.

The End of a Term

MAYA

Abhilasha Ojha

She was seven years old when she performed the role of Bharat Mata (Mother India), for a local nautanki (stage show) in her village. But Maya Bhakuni, the first woman gram pradhan from Boonga – a sleepy, lush-green village of 500-odd families in Uttarakhand – has not only taken this role very seriously over the years, but also polished it thoroughly. Her cheerful laughter echoes in the small room in her home where we are sitting and licking our fingers at lunch – a special hill curry made with gram- and rice-flour, served with rice and salad, in shiny steel plates on a table dressed in a cloth with flower patterns. The room is decked with family photographs. Maya is laughing, covering her mouth self-consciously, when we tell her that we want to write a story on her, on her work – on her as mother, wife and village pradhan. 'Please don't embarrass me,' she chirps, preferring to talk about her childhood and her favourite stage role, one that required her to scream her lungs out ('There are no mikes for these stage shows you know.') and mouth dialogues that would not just entertain but also attempt to educate the village folk on the adverse effects of alcohol, spurious liquor and drugs. 'Not just that, through our plays we also spoke about the need for forest conservation, techniques to preserve water, and safe drinking water,' she says, twisting the end of her magenta sari with bold floral prints. She thinks for a second and then asks me, 'But as someone from the city, will you even understand these problems?'

I am at a loss for words, but thankfully she is already continuing with her childhood story. Hailing from Nahalkot, from an army background (her father was a subedar and her uncles were jawans), Maya, the third of five children, studied till 'Inter' or class 11. She still remembers how her Ija (mother), herself a class five student, used to make her three girls revise their studies in the kitchen while she prepared food. 'She used to give us pieces of coal. We would write on the walls and tell her all that we had learnt during the day, sitting in the kitchen,' remembers Maya. Her Ija would instill confidence in her ('She hated it if we were silent spectators.'), urging her to participate in different plays that she, her husband and brothers-in-law organized in the village on festive occasions. While hordes of people came and watched the shows, admiring little Maya's efforts at attempting the complicated roles of goddesses and mythological characters, there were also voices of dissent, targeted especially at the family. 'There were people who used to tell my father, "Why do you let the girls study? They'll become besharam (shameless)." But my parents always wanted me and my sisters to speak our minds, an attitude rarely seen in most families.'

Maya's tryst with Mother India hasn't come to any conclusive end. 'I was elected unanimously by the village for the post of the village pradhan since I'm a Rajput,' she says with pride. 'Since our family has been very well-respected in the village, I was asked to take up the post.' Is that why she got the position, I question her point blank. 'No,' she shifts uncomfortably, quickly adding, 'I've never taken my role as a pradhan for granted. I've worked hard and tirelessly for five long years.' Over this period, with the able support of her husband and two children (young, handsome boys, who are studying to be a lawyer and engineer in nearby Almora) Maya has faced brick-bats, taunts, furtive glances, a barrage of abuses and accusations about siphoning away the village money.

'Being a woman pradhan isn't difficult. It's thinking independently that's most difficult for people, particularly men, in the villages to swallow,' she says. But none of the criticism has been able to take away either the confidence or the smile that brightens her plump face, her ability to constantly laugh at herself, and to think of even failures as victories.

By that yardstick, the latest 'victory' in Maya's store arrived in the early days of September 2008, barely a couple of weeks before we meet her. This victory has been a bitter defeat, a 'block pramukh' seat that she lost by 50 votes to another candidate – someone who, the Bhukanis believe won by unfair means: bribing villagers and offering them unlimited free liquor. Maya admits that the result came as a rude shock, not because she was overconfident, but because she had believed that people wanted to support her, wanted her to win, wanted her to represent them and address issues at a bigger level. 'I really thought it was the people of my village who wanted me to graduate to another level. My village comprises about 400 families. As a block pramukh, I would have looked after 89 villages, addressed their problems and made a dent somewhere,' she rues, staring into space, visibly upset by the chain of events. But besides all the bribery that played out, could it have been something else, perhaps facets of her own strong personality that cost her the seat? 'I fight openly,' she says. 'Sometimes maybe I come across too strongly in my views.'

Ironically, the voting procedure for the block pramukh took place in the village Chanauda at Briksh Bishar Pathshala, a primary school, the walls of which have been slapped with coats of ecru paint, where her elder son studied and on which she spent two lakh rupees to renovate, construct rooms and increase space for the village children to study. As she prods me to have my tea that her husband Balam Bhakuni has prepared, we step out to the rooftop of her home, from where she points out to a lush green hill where the school rests. 'Not even the gods,' she winks cheerfully, 'could help me win this time.' She laughs once again while I imagine how on the day of the elections 800-odd people would have made their way to the voting booths at 7 a.m. and voted against Maya, and then with folded hands begged forgiveness at a local Shiv temple which rests right in front of the building. 'So many people came home and admitted that they had voted against me and that they regretted the decision as soon as they'd cast their votes,' she says.

Behind all the cheerful spirit and courage that she displays, is Maya disillusioned? 'Of course I am,' she admits immediately, her sharp voice rising in a crescendo. But she clarifies that her grouse is targeted towards people who sold their precious vote for money and booze. 'I knew what was happening as there were stories floating in the village. A lot of people asked me to campaign aggressively, but I refused to throw away money and offer them alcohol – after all, my fight has been against precisely these vices,' she says, glancing cautiously at her husband. He gives a sheepish grin, promising to share some of their personal story a little later. What Maya also abhorred, was the fact that a majority of women who were standing for elections in Uttarakhand didn't even know the magnitude of the responsibility. 'I found it silly,' she says, 'that so many supporters of the opposing party actually went and garlanded the husband and congratulated him instead of his wife who had won the election!' So what was Maya's campaigning tool? 'I love knocking on the doors of people,' she quips, adding, 'I went to everyone and told them not to sleep on the day of voting and asked them to use their minds while voting. I never said "Vote for me."'

The loss of the seat has already changed a lot of things in the Bhakuni household, the most important one being the sudden collapse in the number of people visiting Maya. 'For five years,' grins Balam, 'our home was the pradhan headquarters.' Groups of women, sometimes even men, came to the doorstep, right where we are sitting now watching the verdant landscape, hoping that their pradhan would not only listen to their problems, but also address and solve all their issues. And even as they cried about wayward sons, alcoholic husbands, jobless brothers, ruined crops, water shortage in the farms, lack of green cover, lost cattle, and what have you, Maya never failed to lend them her shoulder to lean. She heard them out, never mind that she did this while doing her own household chores; chopping vegetables, preparing food ('I never let my children or husband go hungry.'), mopping floors, scrubbing utensils and washing clothes. 'She was successful because she was their friend. Maybe that's why she didn't mind not getting even a single minute off for herself,' shrugs Geeta, a member of Mahila Haat, an NGO that has trained Maya and watched her progress as a pradhan at close quarters.

It's no wonder then that even Geeta finds it hard to believe that Maya's home, when we visit it together, wears a deserted look. There's no one sitting on the steps waiting to meet her. Only a still silence, broken occasionally by the chirping of the birds, the sound of raindrops, a sudden swish of the strong wind, or a vehicle honking furiously before racing past the road that overlooks the two-room house. And even as Maya starts her life sans the spotlight that has firmly been on her for the past five years, she says she's starting to love every bit of the slow pace of her life once again. She had given up farming and sold the cattle when her trips to the block office, situated seven kilometres away, increased. 'I couldn't manage looking after so much all by myself. The village development took precedence over family,' she says wryly. Maya's day began at 4 a.m. sharp, followed by cooking, cleaning and feeding her family, after which she trekked, every single day, for two kilometres to be with the villagers. 'My village,' she says, pointing towards a nearby hill, 'is divided into two areas, each area settled around two hills and separated by a kilometre.' Although the villagers used to visit her, Maya invariably trekked across every day to hold meetings, so that all the village women could gather. As if that wasn't arduous enough ('I lost a lot of weight in the last five years,' she jokes), her block committee office in Takula, where all gram pradhans, block committee members and local administrative officers gathered once a month, was situated seven kilometres away. To make things worse, there was no road connectivity between her village and the block office, only potholes and stones, and occasional horror stories of how dangerous the path was for women who travelled alone. These backbreaking journeys notwithstanding, Maya, sometimes accompanied by her husband, sons, or a group of women from her village, claims that she has lost count of the number of times she's paid from her own pocket to hire jeeps to reach the office. 'Once, it started raining very heavily and our jeep couldn't start. Along with some other women, I walked for two hours all the way to the office, only to find that half the staff hadn't even bothered to reach,' she recalls.

Her life now presents a sharp contrast to her life then. How does she feel, now that she's retired? 'I haven't retired,' she clarifies firmly, raising her eyebrows when I question her about her forthcoming projects, and whether they'll be affected at all by the turn of events. 'I have already laid a pipeline of 1,500 metres. Last year, we extended the pipeline by 1,200-odd metres and this year just 200 metres of pipeline work – temporarily stopped because of the harvesting season – will solve a lot of our water problems. Not just that, we've also created many mini check dams for irrigation of the fields.' Maya's struggle for pipeline work (for which she wrote letter after letter to the local authorities to get clearances and funds) has ensured that water reaches all the farms and homes in her village at all times. That apart, she has helped the government sanction 50 lakh rupees for another yojana (plan) that will ensure uninterrupted water supply to reach her village. It goes without saying that Maya will continue to hold workshops with the village women to teach them weaving, embroidery, candle-making, pickle-making and other skills.

But Maya is determined to see that no one starts slacking in forest conservation and preventing the consumption of alcohol and drugs, and the sale of spurious liquor. She regards these as the projects closest to her heart. 'I was sick of people cutting our forests for their kitchens. I used to look at the depleting forest cover and tell my husband that we need to do something,' she says, admitting that it was an area where her interest started way before she became the village pradhan. 'Womenfolk,' she explains animatedly, 'are the ones who usually collect firewood and I decided to speak to them directly.' Being a woman, she felt comfortable discussing the problem with them, although the solution was not easy and required the villagers to go further into the forest to gather fuel. By 2003, Maya had managed to extract a promise from every member of about 400 families that they would not cut kacchi or live trees, and instead get wood from old trees, whose branches had fallen to the ground. A fine of 500 rupees was introduced and Maya's hard work paid off when she once observed her neighbour taunting another family for cutting young trees. 'That embarrassment, the shame of cutting a young tree, finally worked,' she says, happy that with the support of the villagers she's planted around 20,000 trees in the village's main forest area. For the past six years, the village has created a record of sorts by not cutting a single kacchi tree, subsequently expanding the green cover enormously.

Maya believes that trees, especially in the hills, are meant to be worshipped, and once that attitude filtered into the minds of her people, the job became much easier. Today, villagers don't blindly cut trees; they perform a ceremony, pray to them and thank them, take their blessings and then proceed with any cutting that needs to be done. Likewise, Nadi Bachao Aandolan, another project that Maya started five years ago, involved door-to-door campaigning, urging the villagers not to rob the river Kosi of its silt by sand mining, thus creating holes in the riverbed and obstructing its natural flow. 'We are hill folk. For our forest cover to deplete and for our waters to recede is shameful. The forest and water is what we have, what we worship, what we respect.'

Maya's body of work has been vast – a tiny proof is the nahar (stream) that we find running across a farm; the owner waves his hand at us from a distance. She acknowledges him but I can sense that her body is giving away signs of extreme tiredness. She complains of back aches and some throbbing pain in her knees, but would like us to believe it's nothing but old age catching up with her. I shake my head in disbelief, trying to understand why on earth a middle-aged woman would wake up at four each morning to finish her own household chores in order to have the day free for more important work. This includes addressing social gatherings, creating bank accounts for women, helping groups procure subsidies for buying cattle, seeds and tractors, getting transformers installed ('I didn't want flickering bulbs in the name of electricity.'), getting medical vans for people, renovating buildings, and launching women's self-help groups. She walks two kilometres every day to reach the interiors of the village and sometimes hires vehicles with her own money to reach her block office. What is in it for her personally? Why did she push herself every single minute as the voice of her village? Does she now think it was all useless, especially because she lost the number game of politics in the long run, that too by unfair means?

This barrage of questions makes Maya smile even as she stammers to give an immediate response. She says she misses the people thronging her home, asking her for solutions to their problems. 'These are the lessons I've learnt being in politics. Where are the villagers today? Why aren't they here in my home? Why have things changed?' she wonders aloud. But she also adds, 'No development takes place because of one person. Progress can be made only when the people making up society decide to walk along with you, in agreement with your ideas.'

Maya's campaign against spurious liquor and alcoholism in the village has found many allies among the women, being an issue close to their hearts, and is borne out of Maya's personal experience too. Her husband Balam was an alcoholic when he met Maya 24 years ago, and married her after a family friend got the proposal. 'I overheard our friend telling my parents that there's a family, very respectable but with no real foundation. Maya will be able to set them on the right track,' she laughs now, although aghast at that time when her parents gave their consent to the wedding. For three years after her marriage, Maya struggled to keep the family intact, especially because there was tension and a growing distance between her husband and his brothers and sisters. Balam's parents had died when he was a teenager, a primary reason that he cites for plunging into alcoholism. The going only got tougher for Maya. 'As a young girl we used to talk between friends about our future husbands; girls would talk about good looks and rich families. I had just one condition – my future husband shouldn't drink or smoke,' she laughs.

It might be easy for her to laugh after all these years, but as a young bride she shuddered to discover her husband coming home drunk every single night. She cried and cursed her fate, sitting alone in the kitchen, missing her parents' home, her siblings and their laughter and banter. Her father's joint family comprised as many as 15 to 20 people who gathered together for meals. 'I got so lonely suddenly and I wasn't used to it at all,' she says softly. A year after their marriage, she gave birth to her son, and three years after his birth, a second son was born. The younger one was barely a month old when a huge fire broke out, damaging the family shop that Balam managed. Shaken by that episode, and by their critical financial position, Balam once again sought the company of the bottle.

Maya borrowed money from her parents to purchase seeds and cattle, and began managing the farms, along with caring for her two little children, even as Balam shied away from responsibility. 'I was so sick and tired that once when he came home drunk and passed out in the verandah, I just let him be, and in the morning my three-year-old son went to wake him up,' she says, while Balam looks on. He chips in, 'When my son woke me up that morning, I was ashamed of myself.' Although giving up alcohol wasn't easy, Maya's indifference, constant questioning by his own children and a complete breakdown of his family life gradually bailed him out of this habit. 'I don't know how I helped him kick the habit, but yes, I wasn't happy being the sort of woman who would cook and clean even as her husband came home drunk,' she says.

I would learn a lot about Maya the next day, while sitting in the Mahila Haat's humble office. Here I would see facets of this gram pradhan's personality through photographs and local newspaper reports. They almost seem like Maya's progress report card: there are bundles of photographs that feature her holding banners, sitting at dharnas and protests, at 'chakka jams', preparing food for the community at a local picnic, giving speeches, playing Holi, attending Hunger Project seminars... 'She's everywhere,' I joke with the Mahila Haat members, shaking my head in disbelief at the energy that this middle-aged woman exudes. It's her expressions in most of the pictures that catch my eye. She's throwing her head back and laughing at a joke in one, smiling cheerfully in another, raising an eyebrow, gesticulating with her hand in the air in what's clearly an important speech, staring into the far distance as if she's thinking about her next plan of action for the benefit of the village...

Back in her residence, Maya forces us to stay for dinner. She's already in the kitchen, bringing out pots and pans, and fresh vegetables that will have to be chopped for the next meal. I look around her home; it looks comfortable, quiet and peaceful. 'What sort of girl would you like to bring home, didi?' I ask her. Maya's answer is to the point: 'I'd rather they select their own life partners, but I just hope they are girls who think well and are independent.'

In her village, a majority of the boys and girls, Maya reports proudly, complete their graduation at least. 'The girls in our village finish their B.Com and B.Ed too. At least they dream of being teachers, at least they want to secure their own future,' she says. Balam, in a crisp white kurta, is sitting at his ironware shop that he's named – what else – Maya. As we take leave, I turn my gaze to the hill where her village rests. There are tiny lights twinkling in the far distance, evidence of the electricity supply that Maya has ensured for her village. The hill looks so green, I comment, watching Maya flush with pride at another testimony to her efforts in conservation of the forests. She may have lost the recent elections, but the proof of her victory seems to be stamped everywhere, for everyone to see. This Maya is anything but an illusion.

The Ballet Dancer

Maloti

Sonia Faleiro

Maloti Gowalla smoothes the white chador over her green mekhla and in a single fluid movement, gets down on her knees and touches her forehead to the hard, dusty ground. The audience nods appreciatively – she is offering thanks for their presence at the afternoon's gaon panchayat.

Moments before, Maloti was sitting upright, her back cushioned by a bolster, a shot glass of tea in her left hand, in her right the tamul paan she had prepared to her taste from a brass plate of betel leaves, raw betel nut and lime. She chewed on this preparation all afternoon, her chewing a grammar of its own. When she slowed down, or more rarely, paused, she was listening with care. When she ground hard, she was deep in thought, imagining the pros and cons of choices before plucking from them the most suitable ones. Before she bowed to her audience and started speaking, Maloti neatly spat out her wad of paan. This dismissal was an intimation that she was ready to talk business.

'There is much work to be done,' she tells the audience. She describes ongoing projects, including the rebuilding of a dam on the river Sakal. 'Be patient, we are doing the best we can do. But,' she cautions, 'we must all work together if we are to enjoy success.'

Maloti, 42, of Titabar town in Assam's Jorhat district, is an elected member of the No.6 Titabar anchalik panchayat. The anchalik panchayat is particular to Assam and is the intermediate panchayat, above the gaon panchayat, and just below the zilla parishad.

By Titabar standards, Maloti is an old political hand, having been for five years previously the president of the No.83 Namchungi gaon panchayat, and before that, a member of the local mahila samiti. Although Maloti unseated a man for the presidency, she was, at the time, one of seven women panchayat presidents of the district's 17 panchayats. The 73rd Constitutional Amendment is an opportunity the women of Jorhat have embraced. At the gathering that September afternoon, Maloti was one among three women speakers, addressing a little less than a hundred villagers, over half of them women.

The enthusiasm of both Maloti and her audience is, however, tempered. Assam's tribal structure is less patriarchal than mainstream Hindu society,[1] but its history with women in politics hasn't been any less uneasy or dangerous. In the December-January 2007 panchayat elections, the army and paramilitary forces were deployed to ensure fair elections. Yet, re-elections took place in over 166 polling stations. At the time, a 39-year-old tribal woman called Numoli Mesh, won a historic victory by 31 votes in Sonitpur district, contesting not from a quota, but an unreserved general seat. After the win, Numoli was threatened and her supporters roughed up by her defeated

[1] 'Baptism by Fire: Women's Experience of Contesting the Assam Panchayat Elections 2008' by Rahul Bannerjee, The Hunger Project, 2008.

opponent, Robin Basumatary, who filed an application for recount. After the recount, he was declared the winner by 36 votes. Thuggery is inherent to local politics, a terrain littered with violent clashes between leaders representing or supported by political parties such as the Congress and the Asom Gana Parishad (AGP), many of whom see their female opponents as more vulnerable than men, to threats of physical harm.

Maloti's entry into local politics, however, was fluid, even unremarkable. She says her victories at the gaon and anchalik panchayats have increased her status, and won her the respect of the community's men. But her influence comes from something other than votes. A stout woman of medium height, Maloti never leaves home without a red bindi on her forehead, a bamboo fan in her bag, and most importantly, a compulsion to conduct herself with the delicate, if firm, tread of a ballet dancer.

It is a lesson, she says, learnt early in life.

***

'One day, my grandfather gathered my four sisters and two brothers around him,' Maloti recalls. 'I was about seven then.'

> He asked each of us what we would like to be when we grew up. My sister said 'masterji'. My brother said 'doctor'. But I said, 'Grandfather, you tell me what I should become.' He looked at me for a moment and then replied, 'Help your fellow villagers. Not just those who are like you, of your background and caste, but those who are different, worse off. And

help them not with pity in your eyes, which will shame them, but as though what you are doing is for you an honour, your duty. That's the only way to live—by helping those who need it most, and by doing it quietly. Remember he who works hardest should speak softest, and tread most carefully.' Then he added with a laugh. 'Who knows, maybe one day you will even become a mantri!' So that's how the idea came to me. Of helping other people, but quietly, with peace in my voice and gentleness in my actions.

Maloti's grandfather, Anand Gowalla, was an educated and deeply religious Vaishnavite Hindu whose ancestors were Jadavs, originally from Patna in Bihar. In the 1800s when one of them visited the region, he was so taken up by its physical beauty that he decided to stay on. He bought land, planted rice and tended to farm animals. The villagers of Golaghat district, where he settled, were in turn impressed by his wisdom and anointed him gaonburha, village head. Anand Gowalla continued his ancestors' tradition of looking out for others. Each evening he would invite villagers to join him in prayer at the namgarh, prayer hall, built next to the family home. Once a week he would distribute food and clothing to the needy.

When she was 18, Maloti's grandfather and parents introduced her to the man she would marry. Gunadhar Gowalla was 28 and lived and worked on the Chamong Tea Estate in neighbouring Titabur. Six months later they married and Maloti moved into her new home, one that was separate from her in-laws. For two years she was a housewife, gradually adding to what is now a sprawling house with four rooms, a courtyard and namgarh, a cowshed, rice field, and a garden full of flowering trees, herbs and vegetables. Walking through, it is clear that the Gowallas enjoy a contented life and that their house shows the strides that they and their children have made. There is a desktop computer, which Maloti's children use. And a sewing machine she enjoys.

After her first child, a son, was born, Maloti had time left over from her familial duties to turn her attention elsewhere. Even then she showed foresight. 'I noticed how bad the main road that ran through the tea estate was,' she recalls.

> I thought about how difficult it would be for my son to walk or cycle down that road when he was old enough to go to school. And not just my son, as I explained to the other villagers, but their sons and daughters as well. So I thought of paving it. At first no one wanted to help me. 'Why bother?' they would ask. Then one woman did, and then another and another and another, until there were 12 of us young things carrying bricks on our heads—no baskets even!—and paving the road the best we could.

The women who had helped her would become among her strongest supporters when she officially entered panchayat politics.

While Maloti worked, her husband Gunadhar, an overseer on the tea estate, stayed in the background. Even after the road was completed, he never brought it up. He didn't comment on the fact that his wife had displayed an unusual independence in taking on a difficult project. He behaved as though nothing in their lives had changed.

This was, of course, not true. Maloti had gone from being Gunadhar Gowalla's wife to Maloti, the woman who had paved a road. Her actions were inescapable, like dust in the air. They hinted of a new beginning, and of a change that would impact both the village and the Gowallas' family life.

Then several nights later, just when Maloti was beginning to get worried about his silence, Gunadhar turned to her and said in his slow, calm voice, 'You have big ideas. They must be matched with big actions. You should keep working like this.'

'From that night onwards,' beams Maloti, 'he supported me 100 per cent.'

In the background of Maloti's peaceful domesticity, Assam waged war with itself. Since the British won the region from Burma in 1926, it continued a tumultuous history.[2] It was first an appendage of the colonial province of Bengal; its boundaries were redrawn twice, in 1906 and 1912, and following independence, it lost a large part of Muslim-majority Sylhet to Pakistan. Soon after, Bengali Hindus came under attack in a campaign to reiterate 'ethno linguistic Assamese exclusiveness' and in 1979 the 'cleansing rhetoric' against 'foreigners' led to the creation of numerous hard-line groups, as well as political parties like the AGP. After the AGP won the general elections in 1985, but failed to stem the alienation of the tribal and ethnic groups, the rhetoric and actions of the United Liberation Front of Assam (ULFA) developed and hardened. Later,

[2] 'Community, Authenticity, and Autonomy: Insurgence and Institutional Development in India's Northeast' by Jyotirindra Dasgupta, *The Journal of Asian Studies*, Vol. 56, No. 2 (May 1997), pp 345–370.

the Bodo Separatists and the Bodoland Liberation Tigers came into being.

Collectively, these groups have been responsible for blowing up trains and bridges, for bomb blasts, for kidnappings and murders – including, more famously, the kidnapping of the social activist Sanjoy Ghosh in 1997. Ghosh, who headed the non-governmental organization, Association of Voluntary Agencies for Rural Development, was kidnapped from Jorhat where Maloti now lives. She recalls the time vividly.'

'We knew our world was changing,' she says. 'That the peaceful childhood we had enjoyed could be something that would elude our children. Bombs were bursting, people were being shot. There was such chaos. And then they killed this young man.'

Although Ghosh's death disturbed Maloti, it didn't deter her. ULFA's actions hadn't personally impacted her life; no one she knew was either of them, or suffered because of them. And her interest in social welfare was her inheritance, something she had acquired as a child. She said the murder taught her to be careful, but the tea garden cocooned her, and in many ways she was protected from the tumult of this new Assam.

***

In the 1800s, when the British first introduced tea estates into the region now known as Assam; it was a 'rude and insecure' place no one wanted to move to.[3] Planters had to

[3] 'Plantation Economy' by C. R. Fay, *The Economic Journal*, Vol. 46, No. 184 (Dec 1936), pp 620–644.

forcibly obtain and retain labour from the Santhal Parganas of West Bengal and Chhota Nagpur of Bihar in a system with severe penal contracts. Labourers who voluntarily sought work had fled even worse circumstances; the Savaras from Orissa's Ganjam district, for example, escaped 'deep poverty and the frequent attacks of deep-forest animals.'[4]

The Chamong Tea Estate – known locally as the bagaan – was created in 1916, and is now one of four owned by the company in Assam, and 12 in West Bengal's Darjeeling region. It is a 1000 acre village of neat mud houses that run along one side of the verdant gardens. A river runs through the estate and so does a railway track. Children play in the sun, as goats and cows graze in the vegetation of ditches, and hens squawk haphazardly here and there. Despite the tremendous physical labour that takes place here, the village has a somnolent, golden air.

Like most tea estates across Assam – which produces more than 50 per cent of India's tea – Chamong has its own way of life. This relates directly to the British creation of estates in the region. Many of the workers here are descendants of indentured labourers. It is entirely possible that the only shared experiences of two neighbours are of the workplace and of generational poverty. And so, Maloti deals not only with the challenges of working in a village community, but of working in a community within a community. She is particularly concerned that the families of scheduled castes and tribes and other backward castes and minorities are secured from feelings of marginalization.

[4] 'The Savaras of Mancotta: Effects of Wage Labour in Tea on Tribal Life' by R.K. Kar, *Current Anthropology*, Vol. 19, No. 1 (Mar 1978), pp 211–212.

She tells me there are 120 Christian families on the tea estate, and 14 Muslim ones. Tribal representation includes people from the Mising, Das and Kosari tribes. She attempts to include them in panchayat meetings. She solicits their opinion when she takes her daily walk through the estate, and enquires about their welfare.

About 2000 adults live on the tea estate, at least half of whom work in the gardens as permanent or temporary workers, cleaning and manuring the soil, spraying insecticide, weeding, plucking tea leaves and overseeing tea pluckers, as Gunadhar Gowalla does. A permanent worker earns 58-and-a-half rupees a day. A temporary worker earns exactly half that amount. Among permanent workers, there is a distinction, however, with a woman's benefits extending only to herself and her children; while a man's extends to his wife, children and any other family members who may live with him. These benefits include free healthcare – family members are hospitalized when necessary and the bills are paid by Chamong, they receive free medication when it is prescribed by the doctor on the estate – and for the worker, a provident fund. Both permanent and temporary workers receive subsidized rations that cost 50 paisa for three kilos of rice and atta, distributed per person, per week.

Maloti has never worked for Chamong in any capacity. She started her life with Gunadhar as a housewife and would have continued that way had she not decided to work on her grandfather's advice. Gunadhar is the primary wage-earner of the family, and receives 2,500 rupees a month. In addition to health care and rations, he receives every year an umbrella – Assam is one of India's wettest states, after all – a mattress, a set of clothing, blankets, and a saucepan.

It isn't a significant amount, especially now that the Gowalla family has grown. They have three adult sons and two daughters. Most still live with them, and they do all the household chores so that Maloti can concentrate on her panchayat responsibilities. A few months ago, to bolster her panchayat salary of 500 rupees a month, Maloti opened a store in her front yard with an initial investment of 14,000 rupees. It's a typical village store crammed with a vivid mix of goods – black pepper, Colgate tooth paste, 'Pizza' biscuits, sacks of garlic bulbs and peas. Maloti says she's waiting for Gunadhar's annual bonus to make a further investment of about 20,000 rupees. 'You have to invest money to make money,' she says pragmatically.

The poverty on the tea estate isn't obvious – houses are clean and mud-lined, with bamboo roofs – but it is undeniable. Large families have traditionally been favoured, and in some one-room houses live as many as six children with their parents. Since children can only start work at the age of 14, and even then as temporary workers until they turn 18, an average family of eight may have two wage earners. If both are permanent workers, which isn't always the case, the family may draw a monthly income of about 3,000 rupees. On the tea estate, as with life outside, this isn't a sufficient amount.

Maloti is a passionate advocate for higher salaries. She speaks of the co-relation between poverty and illiteracy. The estate's labourers, who are largely illiterate and migrants from impoverished tribal areas, believe their children will follow them into the bagaan. They view education as a waste of money. Although the village school is free, it charges an exam fee equal to a day's salary for a permanent worker on the estate. Parents also need their children's wages. And yet education, Maloti knows, is the labourers' only way out of the tea estate. It will lead to skilled jobs that will raise income, encourage further education, and enable children to integrate with mainstream society outside of the tea estate; to become part of the larger world. There are already examples to follow: Some young men and women have found work as teachers and in the 'defence' (police) elsewhere in Jorhat. One of Maloti's sons studied science, another graduated with a degree in arts. Her daughter pursued a course in computer education from Titabar.

'I had learnt something else from my grandfather,' she says in her thoughtful voice.

She had invited me home for lunch and we sat at her living room table eating rice with homegrown saag and fried arbi, colocassia. Next to my plate Maloti had placed a bowl of lemon slices, salt, and a handful of Bhut Jolokia, Assamese chillies known for their miniature size and fiery taste.

'It's not enough to educate just one person,' she said, spooning rice into her mouth.

> Everyone should be educated. So by the time my son was big enough to enter school, I started to encourage other women to enroll their children. I would go from house to house trying to convince them. But they would say 'Maybe your children will be babus and sahibs and managers. Not ours. Ours will work with us on the estate. So what's the point?' But I didn't stop trying. Yes, I wanted my son to be a bada admi, a big man, but

> I also wanted the children of my neighbours to make something of their lives. How could I solve the problem? The same way I got their men to stop drinking: by teaching them. Alcohol makes men misbehave. Idleness does the same thing to children. Children who don't go to school cause trouble, chew gutka, play cards. So I told their mothers: 'If you send them to school, they'll be out of your hair for a few hours. Then once they return they'll have homework to do. They'll be too tired to cause trouble and you will have peace at home.'

Despite Maloti's dedication, however, this isn't a subject she can influence. As a member of the anchalik panchayat, her responsibilities include education, primary and secondary, as well as adult and non-formal. But she cannot force children into school; she can only help those who are already there. When she was president of the panchayat, for example, she built a boundary wall around the local school's football field, and strengthened the school gate. Although this might appear a small measure, it was an important one. The boundary wall prevented wild animals from the neighbouring forest from entering the school. It stopped children engrossed in a game from running out of the field and onto the main road. It kept the village children safe, and was therefore a success for her.

Maloti must also remember that she lives on the tea estate, her husband is an employee of Chamong, and they don't own the land their house is built on. But she isn't deterred.

The politics of the tea estate impacts other responsibilities as well. Under the Indira Awaaz Yojana (IAY), for example, Maloti as panchayat president funded the construction of hundreds of homes for families living below the poverty line. Outside the tea estate, these houses have been built on land that belongs to the householder. Inside, however, the land is owned by Chamong. Even those who can afford to buy land will not be permitted to do so. Although Chamong insists that householders will not be evicted once they are no longer employed by the company, everyone who has benefitted from the IAY works for the company – in some cases, several members of the family do.

From the road she built with her own hands to her challenges in the present time, Maloti has found unusual ways of dealing with issues. Even before being elected panchayat president, although she was new to the village and the politics of the tea estate, she was able to assess the needs of her community, and find simple but effective ways to address them.

One of her long-term victories has been separating the men of Chamong from their sulai, pungent home-brewed rice beer. 'Alcohol creates ill health and ill temper,' Maloti says, although she has no direct experience in the matter. Gunadhar is a teetotaller and in her own family imbibing alcohol is considered a sin. 'Alcoholics beat their wives and children and create misery,' she says, recounting a story she has often told.

> Last summer during the festival of Bihu, I visited the neighbouring village with some panchayat members. When I entered what did I see that gave me such a shock? The road into the village was full of dead bodies! Men, women, children! All dead! What happened? But when I bent down, I realized they weren't dead at all, they were drunk! The men got drunk and they forced their wives

> to drink, and then no one noticed when the children started drinking. The whole village was out!

'A man should understand when what he's doing isn't right,' she tells me, partly in Hindi, partly in Assamese, chewing tamul paan, forehead crinkled with seriousness.

> But there may be one who still drinks. He beats his wife, screams at his children. His wife comes to me because all the women here are my informants – they trust me. That's another advantage of being a woman, by the way! She says 'Didi, help me.' I go to their house and talk to her man. He may be ashamed, and if so, he will apologize. He may stop. But what if he doesn't? Well, after this first warning, if a man still drinks, I go to the manager of the tea estate, as I mentioned he is a man I know well, and I say, 'This is the situation. Take him off work for a few days, teach him a lesson.' Most men would stop drinking now. But let's say there's one who doesn't. The third warning is the simplest. I call the police. I have the man arrested for causing a disturbance and for violence against his wife. But he has been given three warnings, why? Because I'm a woman. This is how I deal with things. Thoughtfully, with caution. What would a man do in my place? First time he hears there's a drunkard about he'll barge into his house, thrash him, tie him to a chair, call the police. The alcoholic will get no chance to improve; he'll be beaten and humiliated into doing the right thing.

***

In 2001, boosted by the success of her advocacy, Maloti ran for the post of panchayat president. 'I realized that to achieve something big you need power,' she explains. 'You require funds. You have to be able to sign cheques. Otherwise the development you have in mind will never take place.'

Maloti defeated the incumbent president easily. By then she was well-known for her campaigns to encourage early education and to stop alcoholism, and was respected in the village. As president, her suggestions were met with approval, and in the handling of projects she was supported by an experienced panchayat who helped her chart grants-in-aid requests from the state's Consolidated Fund. 'Everyone wants to follow a good leader,' Maloti explains. 'That makes them look good; it helps them do good.' She continues to share an easy, if respectful, camaraderie with these people, and they continue to seek her advice on broad issues.

The biggest project Maloti worked on during that time was Sajal Dhara, a water supply scheme introduced in rural areas by the union government in 2002. With a budget of 25 lakh rupees, Maloti oversaw the construction of five tube wells and 35 taps. She also provided gas connections to widows and built prayer halls. 'I couldn't build a namgarh and not a mosque,' she tells me as she walks with me through the village one afternoon, lac bangles clattering on her wrists. 'I couldn't build a mosque and not a church.'

But her neighbours say Maloti's five-year tenure is also remembered for something else. The year she turned 40 she bought a Hero Honda ladies bicycle. A woman riding a bicycle was a novelty only on the estate. Outside it, women and young girls not only rode bicycles, they drove cars and scooters. But in the insulated world of the bagaan, it had different implications. Historical anthropologist Piya Chatterjee contextualizes the impact of Maloti's bicycle. Referencing tea estates in neighbouring West Bengal, she writes, 'Cycling to work (was) clearly a man's prerogative.'[5] A bicycle 'fundamentally altered the length of a working day,' and because leaf could be strapped on the bicycle, resulted in 'less physical exertion.' But women didn't own bicycles, and it wasn't because they earned less – the men all had to take loans for the purchase. It was simply not socially acceptable for a woman to ride a bicycle, and if she did, she was warned, it would be a cause for shame; she would become an object of amusement.

For Maloti, however, the bicycle became another of her 'different' ways of governing. She would ride through the tea estate and through Titabar to the panchayat office six kilometres away, to meet constituents and nip quickly between construction projects.

'Workmen,' she says to me with a laugh, 'need to be monitored. Otherwise they sit around chewing paan and falling asleep after lunch.'

Just as she wished, Maloti has, with each new election – two so far – been entrusted with greater responsibilities. Now, as a member of the second tier of local governance, the anchalik panchayat, she has access to financial resources from government schemes like the Sampoorna Grameen Rojgar Yogana and the Self Sufficiency Scheme.[6] She is

[5] 'A Time for Tea: Women, Labor and Post/Colonial Politics on an Indian Plantation' by Piya Chatterjee, Duke University Press, 2001; Zubaan, 2003.

[6] 'Panchayat and Rural Development Department: Assam,' www.pnrdassam.nic.in

currently overseeing the reconstruction of two dams in the village, projects collectively worth over 43 lakh rupees. But she champions causes the way she knows best, in her own unusual method. When new families start work on the tea estate, and find their finances a burden, she quietly suggests that they collect armfuls of the protein-rich fern, dhekia, which grows wild in the ditches on either side of the gardens. It is a popular vegetable in Assam, consumed in a number of preparations, and while the villagers won't receive money for it – the Titabar vegetable market functions on barter – they will get rice and pulses. She has also come up with her own solution to enrich the lives of the village children by starting the cultivation of a three kilometre stretch of sasi ghass, a local rubber plant, whose value, when fully grown, is over 20,000 rupees. The profits, she says, will be invested in equipping the village schools with computers.

One day, Maloti says, she wants every home in the village to have educated children who can read under the light of bulbs and drink water from the taps. For that, she knows, she will have to contest the zilla parishad elections after her tenure finishes, and, who knows, perhaps even go further.

'Maybe one day I will fulfill my grandfather's dream and become a mantri,' she says, laughing lightly.

You dream big, I tell her.

She smiles. 'We women have to. Otherwise how will the world work?'

The Mukhiya of Loharpura

Veena

Kalpana Sharma

I do not expect to find a woman who is like a taut wire. Somehow I thought she would be more mellow, more relaxed. Veena Devi talks at the speed of an express train, moving seamlessly from Hindi to Magahi. When she gets really excited, it's the latter. Her face, hands, body and feet all get into the act to make a vehement point or to act out an incident. 'He held the gun to my head', she says dramatically, demonstrating exactly how that happened.

Today, at 36, Veena Devi is a well-respected figure in her community, a mukhiya of Loharpura panchayat in Nawada district of Bihar that comprises 12 tolas (settlements) and four revenue villages. But 23 years ago, at the age of 13, she was just the middle daughter of a poor man living in Bachuara village in Khagariya district, one of the flood-prone and poverty-ridden districts of northern Bihar. Her father, a TB patient, owned just one bigha of land and worked as a sharecropper on other people's fields. He was in no position to educate three daughters and a son. The latter, in any case, was handicapped after a near drowning incident when he was a child. As a result, he was slow, could not speak clearly, and was unable to stand on his own feet.

Veena Devi and her sisters worked with their father and never went to school. 'I went for one or two days', she says. 'But how can you learn when you are hungry?'

Unable to educate them or feed them, the poverty-stricken father could only think of one solution: get his daughters married. But there was no money for dowry. So the older sister got married to an equally poor man through a system called golat, where a brother and sister from one family marry a sister and brother from another. No dowry is involved, as they cancel each other out. Veena Devi's elder sister and her mama (mother's younger brother) got married to a brother and sister from another family.

When it came to Veena Devi, the father once again faced a dilemma. A man in his mid-forties, widowed with two grown sons from the village of Sikandra in Nawada district, offered to marry her. He was a schoolteacher and owned land in the village and in Nawada town. Veena was only 13 years old at that time.

Many in the village criticized her father for considering such a match. But her father said that he had no option, unless the villagers together managed to raise the money for a dowry. Finally, several people from her village met the 'Masterji' and approved of him, said he was a good man. So they were married.

At 13, the newly-wed Veena came to her husband's home in Sikandra village. She shows me a faded framed photograph of a bespectacled man. 'He was very kind to me,' she says. 'He looked after me very well.' They set up home in Nawada, in the house that he had built.

Nawada is a town with a history. Home to Siyaram Tiwary, the famous musician of Dhrupad and Thumri, and only a few hours away from Jayaprakash Narayan's Sarvodaya Ashram, the area has links going back to the beginning of Buddhism and Jainism. But none of this is evident today in its narrow streets where cars, jeeps, buses, rickshaws, bicycles, handcarts and people jostle for space. Around every corner are open piles of garbage, happy hunting grounds for the pigs and dogs that compete for the pickings. The bright green of the numerous stagnant pools of water is accentuated by the dull red of open brick structures all over the city, buildings that appear to be perpetually under construction.

Veena Devi still lives in the two-storey structure built by her husband. There are nine rooms on the ground floor, all rented out, and five on the first floor where she lives with her niece Babita (her older sister's daughter). Babita is in class nine and helps her aunt cook, clean and run the house.

Sitting in the corridor between the rooms on the first floor, Veena Devi points to a large room that is her bedroom. 'We had sacks of dry fruits in this room when my husband was alive,' she says. 'He wanted me to eat well, insisted I drink milk, so that I would be strong.' He also wanted her to study. 'He had hoped I would also do my Matric', she says. So he taught her the alphabet and numbers, knowledge that has helped her overcome at least partially, the handicap she feels on being unlettered.

Veena Devi was married in 1985. By 1987, at the age of 15, she was the mother of a boy, Ram Shankar or Pappu. And before she turned 17, in 1989, her husband died. In the span of just four years, she was bride, mother and widow.

'Those days I was so troubled, I didn't know whether it was day or night,' she says, as she remembers the time after her husband died. 'He had cancer,' she says. 'We took him to a big doctor in Patna. We had to borrow money.' But despite the operation, he did not improve.

> After my husband died, I went to my parent's home. I would come to Nawada every three or four months to collect the rent and my husband's pension, and then go back. I used to get around 400-500 rupees. Bachuara is about 400 km away from here. On these journeys, my father used to come with me. Today I can go alone anywhere, but at that time I was afraid to travel alone.

What persuaded her to eventually return to Nawada?

'My mother-in-law,' says Veena Devi. 'She was a good woman.' She came personally to Bachuara to beg Veena to return. She said people in the village were taunting her for having allowed her daughter-in-law to go away.

But Veena Devi's parents were afraid. What if they torture you, they asked. What if they kill you? How can we be sure you will be looked after?

Ultimately, it wasn't reason but superstition that overcame her fear. In Bachuara, she knew another woman from Nawada who told her, 'Eating even a quarter roti in your in-laws' house is better than eating a whole roti at your parents' home. When you die, your parents will only be able to do a three-day ceremony. Whereas, if you die in your sasural, you will get the full 14 days of mourning and your soul will be at peace.'

She says, 'I thought, even if they kill me, what difference will it make, as my husband is already dead. But I will leave my son with my parents.'

Leaving her son behind was not easy. He was in a boarding school. Every day, Veena Devi would call him from Nawada. And she would send a part of what she got from the rent to her father, to pay for her son's education and expenses. 'He was too poor to manage,' she explains.

Her return from her nehra (parents' home) marked the beginning of her new life. Instead of staying with her mother-in-law in the village, Veena Devi decided to move to the house in Nawada town. But most of the rooms had been rented out. The tenant on the first floor was a man called Mangal Singh (who Veena Devi insists on calling 'criminal' each time his name comes up in the conversation). He was far from an ideal tenant. Not only did he refuse to pay rent for four years, but he also used the fact that his wife's name was also Veena Devi to claim ownership of the house.

Veena Devi had to find a way to get this 'criminal' to move. The woman who helped her out at this point was also the one who 'brought her on the road' ('mujhe road pe layee'). This is a phrase Veena Devi uses repeatedly during the course of our conversation, without fully explaining what she means. It is only after I meet Bharati, that I understand the meaning.

Bharati is a feisty young woman, a midwife, who now lives in Kadirganj, in a couple of small rooms with her mother, her children and her husband. But in the year 2000, when Veena Devi was trying to figure out how to deal with the 'criminal', Bharati was politically involved and lived in Nawada. She convinced Veena Devi that it was the politicians who could help her.

Bharati took Veena Devi to meet Pramila Devi, Member of the Legislative Council (MLC) who belonged to the Rashtriya Janata Dal (RJD), the ruling party at that time in Bihar. She also enrolled her in the local women's organization and persuaded her to join their demonstrations and street protests. 'Women would never step out of their houses,' explains Bharati. 'So when I persuaded women like Veena Devi to come out, they were literally coming out on the road for the first time. That is what the phrase means.'

But even as Veena Devi was getting used to the idea of being 'on the road', she still had to contend with the threats of the 'criminal'. She describes dramatically how she escaped with her life once when on a whim she decided to cross the river and visit her older sister.

> I got to the river and found that all the boats had left. Luckily there was one boatman who agreed to go, but wanted 100 rupees. I agreed to pay him and got into the boat. Meanwhile some other passengers also arrived. So in the end he returned my 100 rupees and took me across. By the time I reached nahar paar (the other side), it was too late to return. So I bought rasgullas for my sister and stayed the night with her.

That night, she says, 25 men with guns came to her house, broke open the door of her room, ransacked it, took the television, the fan, the stabilizers and some of her sarees and left behind a threatening message. 'If I had been there that night, they would have taken me away and either killed me or raped me,' she says.

When she came back after a week and saw what had happened, she was distraught. Her tenants begged her to leave. 'Eat the dahi', they said, 'but please leave the dish in which it is set. If you're not here, these men won't come back.' When she went to the police to complain, no one would believe her.

Finally, she turned to her political connections. An important local politician went with her to the police and told them that if he could prove that the 'criminal' had taken her things, would the police charge him? The police agreed. The politician confronted the 'criminal' and managed to get back some of the stolen goods. He told the man that he would not charge him with the theft if he stopped threatening Veena Devi. Thus, the story ended.

By then, Veena Devi was already in the political system. She knew the local politicians. She was heading one of the women's groups. So in 2001, when the panchayat elections were announced, she was persuaded to stand for them and contest the post of mukhiya. She won, even though she had no experience and no money. 'Bharati and some of us women would go around asking people to vote for me. People would laugh at us. But we had a song that said: 'Even if there is a bullet, or a gun, we will not be afraid. Give us your votes, sisters, don't turn back,' she recounts, giggling at the memory.

So began Veena Devi's journey into local governance, something a woman from the Adrakhi Mahto caste (an economically backward caste or EBC) could never have imagined. By the 2006 elections, half the seats were reserved for women. Yet Veena Devi contested and won both times from 'open' seats that were not reserved for women.

This mukhiya has learned quickly on the job. In 2001, she says, she used to get quite bored being the only woman among several men. She was afraid to speak up. She did not fully understand her duties as a mukhiya. Even the other women in the panchayat would let their husbands do all the talking and the decision-making. Veena Devi proudly asserts that she never depended on any man.

Did the state government not provide any training for women who had entered local self-government for the first time? 'Yes, it did, but what could we learn in 10 minutes?' she asks. They were summoned for a day to Patna, given their bus fares, and asked to sign a muster to confirm that they had come for the training. But in actual fact, they got practically no training.

What she knows now is part instinct, part common sense and partly the result of the intervention of the Hunger Project. 'It is they who taught me everything,' she says gratefully about the NGO's training sessions with the panchayat women. At these sessions she understood her role as a mukhiya and her responsibilities.

Veena Devi recounts how in her first term, she was afraid to ask the Block Development Officer (BDO) about funds for development. She had no idea how much she could ask for. She was worried that she would have to find the money herself, if she asked for schemes that exceeded a small amount. Fortunately for her, the BDO did not exploit her ignorance, but instead, explained to her how she could in fact ask for much more for the work she wanted to do in the villages.

How did she overcome her lack of literacy? Would it not be easy for someone to fool her into signing documents?

'I can recognize numbers,' she says. 'So I know the amount written in any document. I always ask the person to leave it with me overnight. Then I get someone I trust to read it out to me before I sign it,' she replies.

Having learned the ropes in the first five years, the 2006 election was not as difficult, and Veena Devi got elected again. But this time it was from the Loharpura panchayat that included her village of Sikandra. What she was not prepared for was the price you have to pay if you oppose the powerful. 'One of my opponents spent over a lakh rupees. He had lots of money. I went on my own to the constituents to ask for their vote. But I still won.'

The victory was not without problems as she faced, what she calls, one of the biggest 'tensions' of her life. The powerful man she had defeated, filed a criminal case against her, accusing her of the murder of a young man in one of the villages. Veena Devi says she felt helpless and scared. 'But I personally went to the superintendent of police and said to him, "Do you think a poor woman like me would want to arrange for such a murder?"' Luckily for her, the officer believed her story and asked, after investigating, for the charges to be dropped.

Another person who came to her aid at that time was the district magistrate of Nawada, N. Vijaya Lakshmi. When Veena Devi went to her, and conveyed her sense of hopelessness about the situation, Vijaya Lakshmi apparently asked her, 'Who lives in the jungle?'

'The tiger', responded Veena Devi.

'You,' said Vijaya Lakshmi, 'are like a tiger. You will eat up all these people!'

Recalling this, Veena Devi says she was lucky that there were government officers like Vijaya Lakshmi who believed in her and encouraged her, and a police official who was willing to take her at her word. 'Otherwise, Didi, I would have been in jail or fighting court cases.'

Vijaya Lakshmi, she said, would always insist that the women speak.

> She would say that all gents are speaking, so a mahila should speak. I used to refuse to speak. But she would insist I say something. She taught us that dhan daulat (wealth) is sometimes with you and sometimes isn't. No one has it. But a vichar dhara (ideology) is the main thing. I didn't have any money but I, a beggar, a widow, a woman, won elections twice, whereas the person who spent one lakh rupees didn't win. All I did was go from house to house with folded hands. So what worked? The money or the vichar dhara?'

After fighting and winning in two elections, Veena Devi firmly believes that your personal conduct makes a difference in the way people see you.

> I would say to people, 'Don't think of me as a mukhiya. I wash my own dishes, clean my floor, I will wash your dishes when you come to my house, whatever your caste. I will get punya, salvation, if I do this.' Is there another mukhiya who will do this?

So how does she manage to do everything and still do the housework? Veena Devi acknowledges that her niece Babita is a great help. 'I get up at 8 a. m. ('No, 10 a. m.,' interjects Babita with a wicked grin) because I sometimes get to sleep after two at night. People come all the time to the house. Sometimes they bang on my door in the middle of the night. They complain about all kinds of things, a brawl, a drunken fight. I am exhausted. The other day I fainted and had to be taken to hospital and given saline.'

All this while, we have been sitting in her house in Nawada. Babita draws water from the hand pump located in the house to make tea. The conversation is constantly interrupted with Veena Devi insisting that we eat a meal. Get a murgi, she calls out. Get some rice from the market. Will you eat the rice grown in my field, she asks, or do you only eat the rice from the market? Get something sweet, she insists. And samosas. Ki ghatlo? she asks in Magahi. What's the problem? Eventually, despite protestations, the sweets and samosas are brought with tea, and the chicken is organized for dinner on her roof – because by the time it is night there is no electricity. This, I am told, is the normal state of affairs all through the year. Only those who have the money can afford diesel generators or inverters that give them power for a couple of extra hours.

The next day we see the mukhiyaji in action. We set off for Loharpura and Sikandra villages. Veena Devi is dressed in the saree given to her by Congress President Sonia Gandhi at a function felicitating women panchayat leaders, organized by the Hunger Project. She was personally invited by Mrs Gandhi to her residence at 10 Janpath.

The moment we arrive at Loharpura, a crowd surrounds us. And the litany of complaints begins, led by a couple of men who are drunk at mid-day. In the village square, a group of men sit on the ground, gambling. They don't bother to look up when we arrive. The village is full of young men. None of them seems to have any work.

Veena Devi takes us to the school that she is getting built. The original building has only two rooms. The children crowd into them and sit along the corridor. There are over 500 students in this primary and middle school, but only four teachers, including the principal.

As we talk to the teachers, an angry group of parents converges on us. 'Why are our children not getting the mid-day meal?' they shout. Veena Devi is clearly taken aback. She asks the principal why. 'No supplies, mukhiyaji,' he says without any apology. Another man who has been looking at a register in the office comes out. He is the inspector. His job is to check all the 20 schools in the area and give a report. 'None of the schools here serves the mid-day meal,' he admits. Why? 'No supplies from Nawada,' he says.

Even the best of schemes remains on paper in Bihar, where the writ of the Supreme Court mandating that all children in government primary schools be served a hot meal at noon, has no meaning; where 'no supplies' is an accepted euphemism for supplies that are diverted to someone else's home or kitchen, rather than to children for whom it is the only nourishing meal they would get in a day.

Can Veena Devi do anything? She says she is helpless, as the mid-day meal scheme has been handed over to a Shiksha Samiti comprising parents of the children and the school principal. The panchayat has no say in the matter. But as far as the angry parents are concerned, the mukhiya represents authority. They don't seem to care about such details.

We leave Loharpura. Veena Devi is tense and unhappy about what has happened. She is not sure what she can do. But she is determined, she says, to complete the school building so that the children have decent classrooms.

But what about the teachers? Here again, she feels helpless. The matter is out of her hands. The new state government changed an earlier system where local people were trained as teaching assistants, Shiksha Sahayaks, and employed in the local school. Now, all vacancies are centrally determined. As a result, teachers from other districts are assigned to schools like the one in Loharpura and they simply don't turn up.

The school in Sikandra is more impressive. A bright pink double-storey building is bursting with children of all ages. Lucky children. They actually have the required number of teachers, four for the primary school and ten for the middle school. And there is a mid-day meal of khichdi cooked by a Dalit woman from the village. The children run off home to bring the vessels to eat the meal. But where are the uniforms that they are supposed to be given free of charge? 'No supplies.'

The school has no water. The hand pump installed in its courtyard has been vandalized. Even the one inside the storeroom has been destroyed. And the toilets are now empty shells. Their doors have been stolen and the toilet pans broken. 'We need a fence around the school,' says the principal. Development in such circumstances is not easy.

In Sikandra, there are no angry crowds waiting for us, only curious people. They greet the mukhiyaji warmly and ask how she is. Veena Devi responds to each one, as she takes us first to the house where her older stepson lives. This is the house Veena Devi entered when she married his father. The stepson has inherited his father's job and has a share of the house. His uncle occupies the other part.

As we settle down, Saraswati Devi enters and sits near the door. Looking at her, one would imagine she is in her seventies. She has no idea how old she is. What she does know now is that she is a senior citizen. And thanks to Veena Devi, she also knows that she is entitled to a government pension of 100 rupees a month. The mukhiya got all the paper work done for her, she says. But to get the 100 rupees, she has to travel to another village, go to the post office and surrender 10 rupees to the postman before she can get her dues. Corruption, it seems, spares no one.

Veena Devi then takes us to a two-storey structure, still under construction, behind her stepson's house. This is the house she is building for her own son, Pappu. But will Pappu live in it, or run off to the city?

He will live in it, she says. But of course, she cannot be sure, given her son's decision earlier in the year to elope and have a registered wedding without telling either of the families. Pappu, 21, married Sarita, 18, from Sikandra village. Both are still students.

Has she accepted her bahu? She had no choice, she says, and at least she is from the same village and the same caste as them. But Veena Devi regrets that her only son denied her the chance to celebrate his wedding. 'I was so looking forward to having a nice wedding for him. Of course, there would not have been any question of dowry. But I could have invited so many people,' she says wistfully.

Pappu and Sarita live in Sarita's father's house for the moment. And custom prohibits Veena Devi from entering her daughter-in-law's nehra. So she urges us to go and eat lunch there, to meet Sarita and her father and talk to Pappu. But she will not come.

Pappu is enrolled in a college that he never attends. Why? Because the teachers never show up, he says. So how does he hope to graduate? 'The teacher gives us notes and charges 600 rupees for them. All the questions in the exams will come from these notes. So I will pass,' he says. His wife is also in college, but is not sure she will continue. In their bedroom is a gleaming new television and a DVD player. But the village has no electricity. When it comes, it lasts for 15 minutes, occasionally for a couple of hours. They live in the hope that things will improve, a hope not echoed by the emaciated men who are working in the fields bordering the road leading to the village. 'Will things improve in Bihar?' I ask. 'Never,' they say in unison.

The people of Sikandra only have words of praise for their mukhiya. As we stand in the village chowk, people point to the paved lanes and the drains. Their houses don't get flooded any more. She also built a talab (tank) and a canal from the river that brings water to the village. Earlier they had to walk some distance to fetch water. And in a village where there is practically no electricity, they now have four solar streetlights so that people, particularly women, need not be afraid to move about in the dark. Even the Dalit basti has new houses that are being constructed under the Indira Awas Yojana. In this village, no one has any complaints.

So what of the future? Where will she go from here? The political bug has bitten deep. 'I don't mind trying next for zilla parishad, or even the assembly, or even parliament!' says Veena Devi with a broad smile. 'I have a constituency. I know I can win.'

But even as she says this, she acknowledges that she is extremely vulnerable as a widow and a single woman. 'Didi, I have achieved so much, become a mukhiya, but still there is no happiness,' she says. 'I still have a lot of tension. I don't know whether I can do everything people expect from me.'

So far, her own instinctive common sense has held her in good stead. Veena Devi has also been a good learner. In her first term, she had to struggle to understand how the system worked. Interventions, such as the one by the Hunger Project, and a sympathetic BDO and district magistrate helped her make her way. By the time she got to her second term, she already knew the ropes. As a result, there was no hesitation in using the funds available to do things like build the school in Loharpura, or pave the pathways and install solar lights in Sikandra. These schemes are sanctioned by either the state or the central governments. But many women like her are not aware. And given her experience, it is clear that without outside intervention, many elected women leaders will flounder and depend on the men, instead of taking independent decisions the way Veena Devi has been able to do.

Training alone, however, does not equip women to deal with the vested problems of development in India. How can women leaders break through the networks of corruption, which ensure that even the best schemes are not implemented on the ground? The fact that mid-day meals are not served in schools only 15 kilometres away from a district headquarters, illustrates the audacity of corruption.

Where she can create a difference, is in the choices she makes on how to use developmental funds. Veena Devi's decision to build the school, or install the solar streetlights, is a good illustration of this. Such use of funds has benefited the maximum number of people. From talking to her, it is not entirely clear how she made these decisions. But she constantly emphasizes that she believes her position as mukhiya requires her to 'serve' the people.

All politicians speak of 'serving the people'. How long can this woman, a child bride, a widow and now a well-known woman mukhiya, hold on to her convictions in a state where crime and violence are coterminous with politics? In the 2006 panchayat elections in Bihar, according to a study[1], out of 20 cases of gender violence investigated, 12 women who stood for elections were murdered, four were physically attacked, one had a false case registered against her, two were threatened with murder, and one was kidnapped. This is the type of climate in which a woman entering politics in Bihar has to survive. Without support from the family, an organization or a political party, it would be impossible for women, even those as brave as Veena Devi, to negotiate the political minefield.

Veena Devi's experience also underlines the need for women in panchayats to get sustained support, not just a one-time training. Understanding their powers is a first step. How to overcome the many hurdles, especially that of corruption at every level, is an on-going challenge. Others cannot give them answers. But if women leaders know they have someone they can talk to, someone who will be a guide at such times, it could make a difference. In Veena Devi's case, having a sympathetic woman official at the district level during her first term clearly helped and gave her the confidence she needed.

[1] 'Case studies of gender-based violence during Bihar panchayat election 2006' by Rahul Banerjee, the Hunger Project.www.thp.org

In a world where the rules are still made by men, where systems of patriarchy are untouched, where caste and class determine status and the ability to wield power, survival is not easy. Veena Devi's political journey, as she contemplates higher offices, will be fascinating to track, for it will reveal whether and how women like her can remain true to their convictions, despite the obvious pitfalls.

The Night Before the Elections

KENCHAMMA

Manjima Bhattacharjya

Even though it happened 15 years ago, it is a night that everyone remembers vividly – Kenchamma, the elected woman representative I am to meet, her father-in-law Cariappa, and even Srinivas, from the partner NGO Vikasana, who meets us at Birur station and escorts us to Kenchamma's house. Each can recall, as if it was yesterday, the drama that unfolded that winter of 1993, the year the 73rd Constitutional Amendment came into force.

The night before the election was one of those when no one slept and you could cut the tension in the air with a knife. Tense groups of men, crowded in tempos, hid in the shadows. They laid sticks on the floor, covered it with a mat and sat on it, waiting for the violence to erupt. A young Srinivas was amongst them, sitting edgily on the sticks. He had just joined his new job with Vikasana, but this was certainly not what he had bargained for. Srinivas was not new to caste tensions; it was a part of life – just as in hotels, lower caste people were served tea in different cups or breakable earthenware that didn't need washing. He was not oblivious to the backlash either. Just before he left his hometown, Dalit youth had raised a furor when someone had thrown chappals in the Dalit tubewell. But a small local election? That too, an indirect one! Just an internal process where nine members of the panchayat were to elect their 'president' for the term, from among themselves. How could such a small event become such a big issue?

Cariappa remembers how ill he was that night. He had been vomiting all day, and the roughing up and abuse he had faced from the other party when they had paid a visit to his house, had left him weak and drained. Why had he allowed it to happen in the first place, he had wondered. A few months ago, when talks began to select a candidate for the newly-reserved women's seat, Cariappa's daughter-in-law's name came up. Everyone in the village knew and trusted Cariappa the cowherd, who took all the cows of the village to graze every day and returned them safely to their owners, well fed and content. He was polite, dutiful and easy-going. As for the daughter-in-law, she was obedient and did not talk much – that was the general consensus. And so, it was decided – Kenchamma would be the candidate for the reserved women's seat in the panchayat.

'I remember saying no,' Kenchamma recalls. 'But perhaps no one heard.' That night had been especially difficult for her. In the adjacent village, in the house of the son of Anna Basapa Rudrapa (the elder supporting her), she remembered stepping out of her 'prison' to go to the toilet. Twenty-seven years old at the time, Kenchamma looked at the 16 dogs in the compound kept for the last three weeks to guard her and Rudrapa himself, who was sleeping outside their door. As she moved to the toilet with 10-15 members of her group shadowing her for security, she could feel the emotions welling up in her. She had gone through a phase of anger and resentment, wondering why the community, her husband and her father-in-law, had forced this on her. Why she, a non-literate woman who had not stepped out of the house and did not even know the neighbours, had been chosen. The upper caste members of the village who had put her up, did all the paperwork. A certain Mr Gangadhar had provided the 40 rupees for her nomination, which her husband had got done – the papers were brought home for her to sign and had been duly submitted. Before she knew it, she had been elected unanimously. It had been smooth sailing.

The problems started immediately after her election, when some people wanted her to be not just a panchayat ward member, but the president of the panchayat. Why shouldn't an SC woman be in the president's seat, the community asked. Just because it is a general woman's seat, does not mean Dalits cannot sit in it, they bristled. The village divided into two opposing groups of mixed castes, as soon as it was confirmed that Cariappa's daughter-in-law was being put up for the post of president. Rumours of a plan to kidnap Kenchamma before the election, prompted her supporters to urge her father-in-law to send her away somewhere. 'I'll go to my mother's place, not here and there,' Kenchamma decided silently. Later that afternoon, with only her one-year-old baby and the clothes on her back, she took the kutcha road round the back through the forest, caught the bus that went to Chitradurga and left for her mother's home. Around the same time, a fight built up near her house as rumours that she had been kidnapped spread, and the two groups clashed violently.

Kenchamma becomes quiet as she remembers. 'There would have been a murder that day had I been there.' By the time she reached her maternal home at ten that night, a group of her supporters had already arrived. Her gentle father almost fainted at the predicament. Anna Basapa Rudrapa promised her father: she is our daughter too, we'll take care of her. That night they took her to a neighbouring village and kept her in Rudrapa's son's house.

Back home, things had turned upside down. After she was gone,the opposing group gave 3,000 rupees to her husband and his family to prevent her from returning at the time of the elections. Her older children, Keshav, Murty and Veena, whom she had left behind in her mother-in-law's care, were sneakily handed sweets to get them to spill her whereabouts. Her father-in-law had told the supporting group that Kenchamma would step out on the day of the election only if there was police protection. Come home, they had all pleaded with her at one point, we can't bear the tension.

Kenchamma was on the brink of caving in and withdrawing from the elections, but images of the days gone by flashed before her eyes – her caring mother-in-law who had supported her all along and looked after the kids selflessly, her worried father and tense father-in-law. 'I can't step back now,' she thought. 'Even with all that they are saying about me, good or bad. They are doing so much for me, I can't let them down now.' She thought of her ashen-faced father and consoled herself that should she die, he had three other daughters. After all, dying was a real enough threat. A few days earlier, the opposing group had promised her husband's brother arrack, and asked him to murder her on her way to the election – a threat he had actually tried to carry out in a drunken state on the day of the election itself.

In spite of all this, on the day of the elections Kenchamma, escorted by the police, made it into the room where the voting was to be held. It was by raise of hands. Eight out of the 10 members raised their hands for her. Only two were for Ratnamma, the upper caste candidate from the other group. 'You are a Dalit woman, and this means so much for us. Don't leave this place for any reason,' some of her group whispered. 'We have faith in you,' they said. Kenchamma was dumbfounded at her victory and overwhelmed by the procession, celebrations and garlands that followed. Here she was, an illiterate 'madiga' – an abusive term her people were called by, since they carried human refuse on their heads – being elected as president of the panchayat! It was a feeling she couldn't describe.

With the win, things became worse. 'It didn't rain that year,' Kenchamma says quietly. 'They said it was because of me. The gods were unhappy that a Dalit woman presided over the panchayat.'

Then the humiliation began. There were the panchayat meetings itself. First they were held in the school, and then in a rented upper caste house. When Kenchamma started going there, the landlord objected. The meeting venue was changed four times. In one, they threw out the chair and table that Kenchamma had sat on. She was barely allowed to open her mouth at the gatherings during the first four or five months. She felt guilty and embarrassed. What kind of a president was she? No good clothes – going and sitting every day and representing her community, and coming back without saying a word. She didn't even know what a cheque was, at first! She would return from these meetings crying with frustration as she trudged back to her SC/ST side of the village.

Then one day, a turning point came. She was invited for a training session by an NGO that said they wanted to help women like her to know how to be a good panchayat member. She went for it, escorted by her husband. As she made her way back from the training, some of the things they had said echoed in her head: 'Your husband can't guide you.' 'Go to meetings regularly, not only when someone calls you.' 'Be careful before signing.'

So, the next time she asked some questions. 'What is this for?' she asked when told to sign something. 'We need 5,000 rupees for drainage work,' the people replied.

'You do the work, then I will sign the cheque,' she said.

The grumbling began as she started asking more questions and refusing to sign at request. 'We bought you the sweets to keep in your house and feed visitors when you won the elections, and still you are not doing what we want?' It was not easy for them to accept that she would do her own bidding and not listen to them. 'If something goes wrong, the community will question me,' she rationalized. 'I have to do what seems right to me.'

There was so much she wanted to do. But first, she needed a space to work from. She took the consensus of the other members and initiated the building of a Panchayat Bhawan. She got 2 lakh rupees commissioned for the construction, on revenue land that belonged to the temple. More grumbling followed from the upper castes. Chanbasapa (husband of Ratnamma, the losing candidate) alleged that she was constructing her personal house on the site, and even filed an official complaint by sending a blind application in the name of the villagers. The district collector came to investigate and Kenchamma told him plainly, this is not for me. When I am gone, others will sit here. If you think it is not needed, it's okay. She didn't want the Bhawan to be in her name, or have her name inscribed on the walls. All she wanted was a place to hold the meetings, from where she would not be evicted, or her tables and chairs thrown out.

After the building was complete, they tried to get an important person from the zilla parishad to inaugurate it. No one came. 'If you people don't come, I will do it myself,' Kenchamma threatened in frustration. Scared that she might actually do it, they came.

Her confidence grew as more trainings followed, adding to her arsenal. Her literacy skills improved as she learnt along with her children, and attended literacy schemes with the self help group (SHG). 'It was a challenging five years. But I learnt so much.' Kenchamma's eyes light up as she relives flashes of her first term.

> Initially men refused to attend the meetings because they didn't want to be 'below' a Dalit woman – even female members wouldn't come for the meetings. Amidst all the other work – housing, lighting, water, sanitation, which I was determined to improve in the village – there was internal politics. There were the secretaries I had to petition to be transferred – some were uncooperative, some stubborn and some corrupt.

Kenchamma recounts the struggles they fought against local arrack, mobilizing so many tired and angry women, going on the streets and burning packets of liquor. This led to resolutions at the gram sabha leading to the closure of arrack shops. A victory that was short-lived, however. 'When foreign liquor shops made an entry in the village, I had to give licences according to the existing rules and regulations,' she sighs. Moreover, the shadow of caste tensions continued to cloud her term at every turn. 'An adjacent village wanted to build a temple and came to me for help,' she recalls, some hurt still evident in her voice. 'I raised the funds for it and got it passed. In spite of this they did not invite me for the inauguration.'

In those five years, however, Kenchamma with her simple ways and down-to-earth smile, made her way into the hearts of people. Even upper caste folk grudgingly acknowledged that she had cleaned their parts of the town as well as hers; that she had paved roads that went past their houses no less than any others. She would keep in constant touch with the women of the village – chatting as she passed by their houses or joining them in daily chores, lending a hand while cleaning rice or shelling betel nuts. She stayed involved in the lives of people around her. If elders were sitting outside, she would bow and take their blessings, and stop and talk to them for a while. She would contribute her thoughts in her own way, to any discussions going on around her. By the time her term finished, Kenchamma had made a name for herself in the village as a hard worker.

After her term ended in 1999 and it was time for the next round of elections, there was no reserved seat for women in her constituency, only reservation for a general SC seat. Kenchamma wanted to contest and had prepared for it, but then an influential villager Basaraj came to her and said, let someone else from your community have a chance this time – a Dalit man. She agreed. But the candidate who took her place ended up being embroiled in corrupt deals and selling panchayat land that had been kept for community purposes.

> I did a foolish thing. When it was time for the second term I thought that I should take the initiative as an individual candidate, having come so far in five years. But then I thought, I will need money to contest, and that stopped me. In spite of sitting at home, my involvement didn't end. I still went to every meeting.

Anyone could access the panchayat system, she had learnt, and so she would visit, take interest and participate in panchayat affairs.

Outside the binds of the panchayat presidency, life continued as normal for Kenchamma – earning by daily wage labour, shelling betel nuts in the sheds of the big traders and putting her children through school – Kiran (now doing a teacher's training course), Keshavmurthy (doing a diploma in civil engineering) and Veena (doing a nursing course). She also did subsistence farming on the two acres of land they had and participated in the women's SHG that she had always been active in.

Formed about 16 years ago, the SHG had started out small, but became a significant part of the lives of the women and the village. Those were the days of bonded labour – the upper castes never really gave money for household or agricultural work. Food, yes, sometimes maybe clothes, but never money. In the days when all they got was 10-20 rupees for labour, the SHG managed to mobilize 3,000 rupees for a woman's uterus removal operation. Initially the activities of the SHG were opposed by the husbands. But as it began to provide loans to women – to set up tea shops or bangle stores, to marry off daughters, and later for a different scale of development – housing, drainage and lighting – the opposition waned. Manjamma, one of the oldest members of the SHG, remembers that time. 'Dalit women like us never had ornaments or good clothes. But even we purchased minimal gold ornaments that gave us status. We don't stand out as poor low caste women any more.'

'Things have changed for Dalits now.' Cariappa sits with a gamcha on his shoulder and a twinkle in his cataract eyes, reminiscing.

> Earlier we were not allowed into the hotel. We were given coffee in coconut shells that could be thrown, that they didn't have to touch. I saw the Gandhi movement. That's when they started calling us harijan, girijan. It gave us courage to face the abuse and confront the powerful. I remember how I threw a coconut shell once into the hotel owner's face and ran away. With women also... (silence). Earlier we were humiliated all the time, suspicious of our wives, whenever they went out of the house, because we knew what upper caste men did with them. But we couldn't say anything, couldn't protect them. And we took out our frustration on our wives.
>
> After she became president, there was no use for us any more. For two years my son or I used to escort her for the training. My wife would say, don't let her go alone. Once I took her for a training, and they took her inside and closed the door! Without telling her, I came back. My wife used to say let her do it. What she is doing is right. Because of her, our family will get a good name. It wasn't easy. Many days went by without food when she wasn't there in the house.

Kenchamma looks down at her tired hands and swallows his accusations silently.

***

Kenchamma had never really been anything other than a poor Dalit woman, until the fateful election. She never had much of a childhood. The fourth daughter, she was made to drop out of school in class three, as her father wanted her brother to study. The daughters dug wells, moved earth and worked in agricultural fields to earn money. 'I haven't really seen any good days or happy times at my mother's place. Even here, I can't say it's been good.' It was an arranged marriage to Shivan, her husband, when she was about 18 years old. Although they have some land, they don't have the irrigation facility – the Gangakalyana scheme for SC/STs in Karnataka provides for one bore-well for every eight acres of land. Kenchamma falls short by six acres and cannot avail of the benefit. Thus her husband goes to graze cattle or to do coolie work, although his drinking problem, like other men in the village, sometimes leaves him incapable of working. On their two acres, Kenchamma grows ragi, paddy, green chillies, a little bit of this and that, for home consumption.

***

By 2003, time for the third round of polling, the villagers had become election savvy. The bitterness and tension, evident in the first term, had given way to a business-like approach to panchayat politics and a new format, called syndicate campaigning. 'Nowadays the way elections are held has changed. A set of people are elected rather than one person,' reflects Kenchamma. It works like a package deal – the voter selects a combination, not an individual – a set of candidates is selected for various posts by groups in the village. One of the benefits is that weaker individual members like Kenchamma don't have to spend on campaigning. For an individual, the cost of standing for elections can be prohibitive, often running into lakhs of rupees. Through the campaigning, people drink, eat and make merry at the candidate's cost. 'Elections mean they are there from morning to evening, and expect morning coffee up to dinner to be taken care of by the candidate,' says Kenchamma.

This time round was no less exciting for Kenchamma. Even as discussions were on within her group that they should give the chance to her sister-in-law Chenamma, a rival group approached Chenamma and announced her as their candidate. Affronted, but not to be dissuaded, the group fell back on Kenchamma. When we have butter in our hands, why think of ghee, they said. Tense weeks followed and the family was divided between their two contesting members. There came a point when the two sides would not even speak to one another, such was the high level of animosity. Kenchamma won the election, but suffered heartbreak over the dispute within the family.

In her second term as president, ten years after her first entry into politics, Kenchamma was prepared. The acronyms all made sense and she knew how to make things work. She knew the needs of her village. She had an agenda and she had learnt how to articulate it. There is an assuredness in her voice as she begins to speak about the major issues in her area.

Caste is the biggest problem in the area. It boils our blood when they all talk caste, especially in front of our children.

The main hospital is 70 kilometres away and you have to take an inter-city train to get there. There is a health centre in the village – but there are never any doctors. It is a posting for new doctors, who usually leave within one-and-a-half-months to go off for higher studies. So at any given time, there is hardly anyone there. Now a government doctor has been deputed three times a week to come and sit at the centre.

Our ration depot is famous in Tarikere taluk. It has three branches, which are open throughout the month, unlike others. Each card holder has a quota, so they get their ration and don't have to face being told that 'ration is over', nor do they have to submit to the black market.

The Karnataka Government Yeshaswini Cooperative Farmers Health Care Scheme is also popular. It is an individual insurance scheme in which people pay 130 rupees a year for health insurance, under which even surgeries and hospital stays are covered. I myself haven't used it, but others have, and it is making a difference.

I try to promote the NREGS but because it pays 74 rupees per day, people opt not to go. Shelling betel nuts allows them to make 200-250 rupees a day.

Quite far removed from the Kenchamma of 1993, who cried in humiliation as she returned from her first meetings, bewildered and frustrated at not being able to say anything. We are walking through the village and my eyes fall on her callused hands. She points to the skin of betel nut strewn in piles everywhere. She did four sacks yesterday. At 50 rupees a box, she made 200 rupees for the day. An old man stops to have a chat. 'Good that reservation happened. In my time women used to go around with their heads covered, stay at home, or only work in their fields at home. Now look.'

Indeed, look. Kenchamma sits in her office on her blue chair, with the plastic cover intact, at the Panchayat Bhawan she got built in her first term. A plaque on the desk says 'Vice President'. Due to a new rotation system, the president and vice president change positions halfway through their terms. So Kenchamma has been president for two-and-a-half years and is now the vice president. Manjamma is the president, but she doesn't come to the office much or take interest in the affairs of the panchayat – at least not without her husband. Kenchamma is not too keen to discuss Manjamma's performance, but it is evident that she is nowhere near Kenchamma's level of involvement or leadership. This is also what comes with syndicate campaigning.

The secretary sits two seats away and takes an important call. 'Yes sir, hello sir... No the president is not there but the vice president is...' he says, handing Kenchamma the phone.

The secretary has been posted here for one-and-a-half years. In his previous post, 8 out of the 16 members were ladies. He thinks for a bit about the changes he has seen over his many years of service. From the first, to the second, to the third batch, there has been an improvement, he says. Now they are more literate and have studied at least up to class four or five. Non-literate women are still puppets in the hands of their husbands, he feels, but there is a difference between the non-literate women now, and then.

This is a moot point. How important is literacy to being a good panchayat member? There is an opinion among many ground workers who build the capacities of these elected representatives that in fact, there is no correlation. To the contrary, literacy usually leads to more corruption. Then there is the other touchy question. Can poor people really be leaders? Those who don't even have sufficient food for a day, how will they manage panchayat affairs? Their very appearance is different, they come to panchayat meetings dressed in whatever clothes they have. They don't look tip-top, like a leader. The final unsaid question also lingers in the air. Do women really do anything differently?

Madapala Lingayat, an upper caste panchayat member since 2003, thinks the agenda of women members is different. The topics they raise are water, cleanliness and sanitation. Men raise issues like drainage and roads. Women notice the small things that men would not notice... if there is a tap or tank leaking, or water collecting somewhere. 'Women are almost equal to men now,' he says. 'First they would not be able to talk to officials, but now they sit almost equally. Now if only, violence against women by women stops, all the problems would be finished.' Women have interest in taking their career forward and working outside their villages and panchayats, but the husbands don't allow them. This needs to be stopped, he feels. Husbands need a broader mentality and women need to be supported.

As for Kenchamma, he is all praises. It is due to the village support, the labour support and of course her own nature, her character. She is a helpful personality. He shakes his head, as if ruing fate. She was born to her community by mistake. She should stand for taluk and zilla level posts next time. She will have 100 per cent support from me, although there may be some opposition from others, he says. She hasn't changed, he reiterates. She hasn't even plastered her house. She still comes for daily wages. He goes inside and takes out three registers to show us her account as daily wage labour in his plantation.

Echoes of these observations are everywhere.

Kenchamma is a good worker.
She hasn't changed.
It is evident from her house. It isn't even plastered.

These echoes stay with me uncomfortably, as I watch Kenchamma wrap up some work at the massive desk she shares with the absent Manjamma and the secretary, and later, as I go through the motions of getting a group photograph clicked. Of course, there is change everywhere for all to see. An uneducated Dalit woman has done for her village what seasoned political aspirants have not. But what has she got in return? What does one make of this strange sort of limbo? Things have changed so much over one generation – from Cariappa's to his daughter-in-law's – yet they remain disturbingly unchanged.

Kenchamma has been president of the panchayat twice and is now a grudgingly-respected member of the village community – respected by both Dalits and Lingayats. But she is still the poor Dalit woman. As if being any other way would be improper. Improper *not* to live in a thatched, leaking, mud hut, or to plaster her house, to *not* struggle for daily wages, improper to imagine other livelihoods, work not just for the village but make a career out of governance and use the 10 years of hands-on learning she has had. The boundaries have been pushed, but still only from the limits of the home to the village. Isn't it enough that you have been allowed to reach this far, the voices seem to suggest? Now you want to step outside the village? Govern other talukas? Even the district? Every stereotype of women's struggles seems to dance in the shadows: Women have to work twice as hard, at the end of the day a woman's place is in the home, women cannot be too ambitious, how dare a woman – a Dalit woman, a poor woman, an uneducated woman – even think of dreaming bigger? They should know their place, stay within their limits.

As my troubled eyes meet Kenchamma's calming gaze over the desk, it is almost as though she knows what I am thinking. For one second, there is no translation assistance necessary; hope flickers and we both smile a half smile in unison, as if in acknowledgement of the fact that this is still only half of our journey. Limits are what women's lives are about, and who is to say that this limit will not soon be crossed?

About the Authors

Indira Maya Ganesh works independently, taking on writing and research assignments on gender, sexuality and HIV/AIDS, culture, media and technology for a range of national and international agencies. She also consults with the United Nations Children's fund, UNICEF, producing training and communications tools and materials for their gender programming with adolescent girls, and their HIV/AIDS programs with young people. She lives and works in Mumbai, India.

Tishani Doshi was born in Madras, in 1975. She got her Master's in writing from the Johns Hopkins University in America and worked in London in advertising before returning to India in 2001 to work with the choreographer Chandralekha, with whom she performed on many national and international stages. An avid traveller, she has been trekking in the Ethiopian Bale Mountains, visited Antarctica with a group of high-school students, gone to read poetry in Cartagena, and been to the village of Koovakam to document the largest transvestite gathering in India. She has written about her travels in newspapers such as the *Guardian*, the *International Herald Tribune* and the *Financial Times*.

In 2006, her book of poems, *Countries of the Body,* won the Forward Prize for best first collection. Her first novel, *The Pleasure Seekers,* is forthcoming.

Manju Kapur is a well-known novelist and a professor of English at Miranda House in Delhi. Her first novel, *Difficult Daughters* (1998), received the Commonwealth Award for first novel in the Eurasian region. She is also the author of *A Married Woman* (2002), *Home* (2006), and *The Immigrant* (2008).

Abhilasha Ojha is features editor with *Business Standard,* a leading financial daily. She follows the media & entertainment beat but thoroughly enjoys working on social sector stories too. When she's not writing, she sings, writes and composes music, takes summer workshop classes for kids and enrolls herself in theatre workshops. She enjoys cooking – once in a while – and eating – all the time. She constantly dreams of ultra luxurious spa holidays, fetching, at the very least, one Filmfare award, writing a book and singing one song for A.R. Rahman in his Chennai studio. She lives in Delhi with her husband and her pet dog/child Foxie.

Sonia Faleiro is an award winning journalist and writer. She is the author of *The Girl* (2006) and a contributor to *AIDS Sutra, Untold Stories from India* (2008). Her first work of non-fiction, about the lives of Bombay's bar dancers, is forthcoming in 2010 and will be translated into several languages.

Kalpana Sharma is an independent journalist and columnist based in Mumbai who writes on environmental and developmental issues and gender. In a journalistic career of over three decades, she has held senior positions in leading Indian newspapers including the *Indian Express*, the *Times of India* and the *Hindu*. She is the author of *Rediscovering Dharavi: Stories from Asia's Largest Slum* and has co-edited with Ammu Joseph, *Whose News? The Media and Women's Issues* and *Terror Counter-Terror: Women Speak Out*.

Manjima Bhattacharjya is an independent writer, researcher and consultant with NGOs from across the world. She has a PhD in Sociology from Jawaharlal Nehru University, New Delhi. She has worked with JAGORI, a Delhi-based NGO working on women's rights and the Women's International League for Peace and Freedom, WILPF, one of the oldest women's peace organizations in the world. She writes for various publications as well as a monthly column on feminism's 'Third Wave' for www.infochangeindia.org. She lives in Mumbai.

Acknowledgements

Thanks to all the women sarpanchs who opened up their homes and hearts to the writers and told their stories.

To the writers who most graciously gave their time, energy and skills to the project.

To all those who accompanied the authors to the field, gave insights in the field and provided valuable translation assistance: Aradhana Nanda (THP Orissa), Sukanto Mohapatra (Lok Adhikar Samukhya, Bhawanipatna, Orissa), Jatindra Mund (Bishwanathpur College, Bhawanipatna, Orissa), Lalitha (THP Tamil Nadu), Perumal and Dhanalakshmi (ARCOD, Tamil Nadu), Shibani Sharma (THP Madhya Pradesh), Geetha (Mahila Haat, Uttarakhand), Tasaduk Ariful Hussain, Rekhamoni and Pubali (NEST, Assam), Shahina (THP Bihar), Shailaja S. (THP Karnataka), and Srinivasan (VIKASANA, Karnataka).

To the state offices and partners of the Hunger Project for logistical support in arranging for the visits.

To all of the wonderful team at the Hunger Project's New Delhi office, especially Sriparna Ganguly Chaudhuri who dreamed up and drove this mission, Rita Sarin who believed in it, Radha Khan and the rest of the team who pitched in happily to make it all happen.

To the Swiss Agency for Development and Cooperation (SDC) for supporting this book in partnership with The Hunger Project; and to Sheema Mookherjee and the team at HarperCollins India for taking on this unusual offering with such enthusiasm and bringing it to its logical conclusion.

References

Aalochana, 1995. *And Who Will Make The Chapatis? A Study of All Women Panchayats in Maharashtra* (mimeo).

Bacchetta, Paola, 2003. *Gender in the Hindu Nation: RSS Women as Ideologists*. Women Unlimited (an imprint of Kali for Women), New Delhi.

Datta, Bishakha (ed), 2001. *And Who Will Make The Chapatis? A Study of All Women Panchayats in Maharashtra*. Stree Publications, Kolkata.

Dugger, Celia W., 1999. 'A Woman's Place: a special report; Lower-Caste Women Turn Village Rule Upside Down', *The New York Times*, May 3, 1999. http://www.nytimes.com/1999/05/03/world/a-woman-s-place-a-special-report-lower-caste-women-turn-village-rule-upside-down.html?pagewanted=all

Ghimire, Durga, 2006. *South Asian Situation on Women in Politics*, paper presented at the 6th Asia Pacific Congress on Political Empowerment of Women, February 2006, Manila. http://www.capwip.org/paperscongress/southasiansituationdurga.doc

Sehgal, Rashme, 2008. *Panchayat women no longer need sarpanch patis*, Infochange News and Features, March 2008 http://infochangeindia.org/200803246988/Women/News/Panchayat-women-no-longer-need-sarpanch-patis.html

Sen, Atreyee, 2008. *Shiv Sena Women: Violence and Communalism in a Bombay Slum*. Zubaan, New Delhi.

Sharma, Kumud, 1998. 'Transformative Politics: Dimensions of Women's Participation in Panchayati Raj', *Indian Journal of Gender Studies*, March 1998, Vol. 5, No. 1: 23–47.

SUTRA, 1995. A Report on the work done by SUTRA during the year 1994 with women members of Gram Panchayats. Jagjit Nagar: Society for Social Uplift Through Rural Action (mimeo).